Circle

Of

Death

Thomas Habersham

Contact the author: Thomashabersham4@gmail.com

Contact TMA Publishing
www.tmapublishing.com
tma@tmapublishing.com
1-855-716-1507

ISBN: 0615635316

ISBN-13:9780615635316

DEDICATION

For Rosa, Cedrick, Alex, Pudgy, Trayon, Trayonna, Aaron, and Javonte; each possessing in some way a part of me. For Laverne, assisting me financially. I couldn't have done it without you.

INTRODUCTION

I published UNPROTECTED SEX in 2008. Shortly after the manuscript was submitted, I began my study in creative writing with STRATFORD CAREER INSTITUTE, outgrowing the style in which the manuscript had been composed. While I had no desire to write a second book of a similar nature, a sequel was promised to the world. Readers questioned my reasons for ending the story the way I had, subsequently questioning the story's conclusion. Others have outright expressed their anger at the jilt. To those I would simply assure the coming of a rectifying sequel, a task I didn't look forward to. Such occasions and encounters were sparse in the beginning, but as more copies were sold, and I received emails, letters, and endured even more encounters with like-minded readers, it was clear I had to deliver.

STRATFORD appointed me an instructor, Meredith Nixon, who tolerated my preferred style while encouraging me to excel. Through Meredith, and other authors I studied under at STRATFORD, I came to understand what I had done to the readers of UNPROTECTED SEX and why that must be avoided. Having outgrown the style in question, and having decided there would be no sequel, the readers would forever know the in-satiated sense I'd giving them. But these weren't mere readers, I realized; they were fans who had invested. With that, it remained my duty, as their author, to provide them a proper climax. Even so, I wasn't up to going through with the original sequel. With that I

altered the script, and the results are what you have here-
to sate those who were formerly unsated. To make further
amends, I offer this book free to those who purchased
UNPROTECTED SEX. Having properly rectified my error,
here is UNPROTECTED SEX's conclusion; CIRCLE OF
DEATH. Enjoy.

DEAR DIARY,

Every six months or so I drop by the clinic to have myself tested, and so it was two weeks ago. Yesterday I returned for my results, but wish I hadn't, having tested positive for HIV. I will confess my love for sex, however, but I was never wild with it. I didn't sleep with just anyone. My aim had always been at steady relationships, in holding true to fidelity.

That said, it can only be my boyfriend, David, from whom this disease has been contracted. That he hadn't come into our relationship with the virus, I'm sure, for we were tested together twice before. Which means he is seeing someone behind my back. Worse, he is doing so without protection, and the implication sets my blood to fire! I've contemplated retaliation, but nothing sure comes to mind. Moments ago, I called him and demanded a meeting in person. He claims to be at home currently working on a project, that he'd come over thereafter. This is a matter which can wait no longer. I've had time enough to think and I want to confront him with this now. I am all set now to go over to his apartment. I can only imagine what I'd have to document upon my return.

DEAR DIARY,

My intent had been to go over to David's apartment and present him with the news of my diagnosis, that which is his now as well. Having been tested together twice with negative results, I wanted to see if he'd try to flip the script and point the finger at me. I also wanted to witness the terror in his eyes as he accepted the news.

I knew firsthand what he'd feel. Knowing death so intimately wreaks havoc on the soul while upsetting the physical. Since obtaining those results, my heart has maintained an accelerated pace with a seemingly constant flow of adrenaline that keeps my stomach quivering with a panicking sense of doom. I've known no sensation in life that equates to this.

I had possession of David's .38 special, which he'd come into the habit of leaving with me. I was going to put a bullet in his head after sharing the dreadful news, but the scenario didn't play out in reality the way it had in mind. As I used my key to enter his apartment, it caught me that he wasn't alone. Feminine excitement, clinking metal, and the heavy slap of flesh came clear from the bedroom. The son of a bitch was in there fucking after telling me he was finishing up work!

Then it struck me how trusting I'd been with him. I wondered how often I'd been deceived in that manner. The idea had me furious! Even if I hadn't gone there to kill him, that would have done it. Even if there was some small chance he would have confessed to his mistake, plead for forgiveness, and somehow convince me not to kill him, it was, at that moment, out of the question. My mind was set; he was going to die. There was no way in hell he could flip the script. He was caught in the act.

I locked the front door behind me and pulled the .38 from my waist, creeping through the front room and down the hall to stand near the open bedroom door. I listened and visualized the proceedings. The girl moaned, and David groaned, their expressions punctuated by the sharp slap of flesh and the woman's coinciding scream. The metallic clink was prevalent, and it was curiosity that compelled me off the wall and in the doorway.

The woman was on her knees and handcuffed to the metal headboard to which she grasped. David had a hold to her waist in taking her from behind. He slapped her periodically across the ass, and she cried out ecstatically. The cuffs clattered and clinked against the bars in time to his stroke.

I felt neither hurt, anger, nor jealous in witnessing the act. However, I will admit to never having seen David perform so aggressively. I didn't think he had that in him. He was seriously giving it to the girl! In contrast, he'd only given me gentle love making. Was all his slow consideration an extended gesture to me and not his true preference? He always told me I was a good girl, his angel. Is that why he sexed me so tender? Is that why he cheated? Did he desire a more aggressive session he felt I wouldn't accommodate nor accept?

I am a good girl when it comes to being utterly faithful, but I am not opposed to what some may call adverse sex. He had only to ask or simply approach with it and he would have found me as accommodating as ever. More so depending on what he wanted.

Though jealousy was absent, I knew rage at having been inexcusably betrayed. Not with the fact he cheated, but for the way he'd disrespected me in having unprotected sex and having brought me this incurable disease.

"Do it harder," the girl said, oblivious to my presence.

David slapped the girl hard across her ass, and she cried out.

"No!" she complained. "Fuck me harder."

David obliged the girl's request and drilled her something fierce. I found myself pointing the .38 at the back of David's head, the hammer cocked. I wanted to kill him right in the act, but I decided to let them finish or note my presence.

The girl climaxed loudly, as did David seconds later, pulling out and skeeting all over the girl's ass and back. The fact he wore no condom infuriated me to the brink of no return. The revolver shook in my hand as I fought for control.

"You fuck everything raw, David?" I said to his back.

They turned simultaneously. The girl flopped to one side

and spun as far as her bonds would permit. David, erection in hand, turned, spotted the weapon and fell back onto the girl's twisted pose. Neither moved nor spoke. Hell, what could he say? He was caught in the act.

"I asked you a question, David, and I expect an answer. Do you fuck everything raw?"

"Not everything," he replied.

"Not everything? Un-cuff her and switch places. I want you on your back."

"Baby–" he began, but I cut him off.

"No questions. No excuses. No begging. Just do like the fuck I say, or I start blasting in this motha fucker! And it's taking every ounce of control not to do so now. So don't push. Don't even try." I pointed the gun at the girl. "That means you too. Are we clear on that?"

The girl in her half-turned position was seriously afraid. I could see it in her eyes even though she tried to maintain a blank expression while keeping her voice neutral with her reply. David released the girl and was cuffed in her place. I commanded her out of the room and told her to proceed ahead of me down the hall. In the kitchen, I instructed her to grab a butcher knife. She glanced back at me then, her eyes more fearful than before.

"Please," she began, but was also cut short.

"I'm not trying to hear anything you have to say," I told her. "So just shut up and let's get this done."

David made a kicking attempt to sit upright as we entered the room and he caught sight of the knife. The cuffs rattled violently but wouldn't accommodate his effort.

"Straddle him," I said to the girl, and her face was a

mask of confusion.

"Strangle him?"

"I said straddle him, stupid bitch! Get on him like you're riding his dick. I'm sure you've done that before."

The girl glared at me for long seconds. Had the circumstance been even, I think she definitely would have tried me. I couldn't blame her, though. I, too, would have been seriously pissed had the situation been reversed. However, I had the upper hand and was quick to remind her of that.

Knife in hand, the girl complied with my directive. David's eyes were twin pools of terror, shifting from me, the girl, the knife, and back again. Blood would be drawn, he knew, and the fact I was calm with the proceedings elevated his fear. My silence bespoke my mind and knowing not my intent is what terrified him most.

"Angel, baby," his eyes were pleading. "Can we at least talk about it?"

I stood near the bedside and kept my distance from the girl and my eyes on the knife. "I'm not your angel," I told him. "And there's nothing to talk about. There's no excuse for your carelessness, and sorry can't change the reality of what you have given me. So just lay there and be the fuck quiet!"

The girl looked on with growing apprehension. I questioned her and she told me her name was Jasmine. She was twenty-two years of age and had been seeing David for just over two weeks. The revelation was startling. Clear it was the girl hadn't been the one from whom the virus had been contracted. I knew a moment's sympathy for the girl, and for a second, I considered altering my intent.

"This is going to be easier than I thought," I told her, "Though more distressing for you, Jasmine."

She asked for clarification, and I proceeded to explain that I'd come to deal with David. But in finding her there I would force her at gunpoint to punish him severely.

"Okay," the girl asked. "What's now to make that easier, but more distressing for me?"

The girl was innocent. A victim like me. I honestly took no pleasure in breaking the news to her, but I explained how I'd initially thought her responsible for what David had given me, my understanding of how that couldn't be the case considering their liaison was only that of two weeks. As I spoke, Jasmine eyes became distant, her face the very definition of horror. I felt sorry for the girl. Her look of trepidation tore at my soul. It wasn't her face I wanted to see reflecting those emotions. I turned to David and was gratified. Though I hadn't said what he'd given me, I was quite certain he had an idea.

"So," Jasmine said, her voice barely audible. "What exactly did he give you?"

I stared at the girl, pained at what her eyes revealed. "From the look on your face, honey, I think you know already. But if you must hear it," I turned my gaze to David, "he gave me HIV."

At that, his expression was everything I wanted it to be. In a matter of seconds I watched him die in every sense but the physical.

"Distressful," I said to Jasmine, although I knew there was no further need for explanation. "In that you would know of your infection; that you were without such before sleeping with David. Easier comes with comprehending the death sentence he's passed on to you, that I wouldn't have to force your hand to punish him."

Having eyed me throughout, Jasmine nodded contemplatively and turned a hateful gaze on David. The knife, near her thigh until that moment, was clutched tightly at her breast. She bowed her head and trembled visibly. I realized she cried, and I felt her pain as only one could in sharing a similar fate. I was suddenly reminded of a tortured child and was tempted to offer a comforting hand of support, but I stayed my ground. If she was even half as distraught as I had been at discovering my diagnosis, she would strike out at any and everything. I wasn't going anywhere within striking distance of her and that knife.

I waited patiently, knowing firsthand the emotional phases she'd go through, the state of rage she'd inevitably come into. I knew the second it arrived. Her head lifted and she locked gazes with David. He knew it, also, having seen it in her eyes. His face contorted with renewed terror.

"Don't listen to her, Jasmine," he said, eyes wide in panic. "She's just trying to manipulate you into doing her dirty work. Don't do it Jasmine. Please! She's angry at catching me− catching us."

"Nigga, shut the fuck up!" Jasmine shouted and feinted with the knife. David bucked beneath her and screamed. The cuffs clinked and rattled against the bars as his instinctive efforts were halted. He went still, gazing fearfully at the knife.

"You think I'm stupid?" the girl went on. "you said you had an open relationship. So why in hell would she be so pissed at catching us? It's not like we're at her place or in her bed— you lying son of a bitch!" She feinted again. David bucked, cried out and fought against his bonds to fend off the feared attack.

"Besides," she continued. "The girl has a gun, David. A fucking gun! That means she had very serious intentions before she walked in on us! How the hell do you explain that, David?"

Although she pointed irrefutable facts, it was my understanding she harbored some hope of him countering with some reasonable explanation. To this, however, he could offer nothing other than silence, and she nodded knowingly. "Just like I thought!" Her voice was venom coated, and when next she raised the knife, I knew it was for real. David knew as well. He bucked dramatically and screamed bloody murder even as the blade descended.

The knife tore through the top portion of his ear, severed a chunk from his skull, and penetrated the mattress. Blood pooled and stained the sheets in a growing puddle of red. His scream of terror became one of pain.

Jasmine wasn't playing with him. His eye had been her target, a blow that would have brought immediate death if he hadn't jerked aside at the last moment. His reprieve was short, however, for Jasmine wrenched the blade free and feinted again. David, hollering like the bitch he was, jerked reflexively as Jasmine, timing the move, brought the knife down blindingly, catching him dead in the throat. His scream was silenced; blood spurted and splattered onto Jasmine's naked breasts. Eyes bulging, his feet kicking violently as he underwent an excruciating suffocation. His face contorted and it was obvious he suffered more from the abrupt deprivation than from the blow itself.

It was my first time witnessing real violence. I didn't blink! I felt satisfaction at witnessing his murder. It didn't stop there, though. Jasmine snatched the blade free and blood surged from the wound to spill over his torso. The knife was raised high overhead and brought down hard into his chest, buried to the hilt. His mouth flew open wide, but no sound came forth, only a gurgle of bubbling blood at the hole in his throat. Consumed by rage, cursing and crying alike, Jasmine riddled David's torso until his kicking convulsion subsided and he lay unmoving beneath her.

Jasmine went still as well, her head bowed, her breathing heavy, her hands still clutching the knife embedded in David's chest. Whether she was in a state of shock, or attempting to regain her composure, I couldn't say. Whatever the case, I took full advantage, closing in to grab a fist full of her hair. I pressed the barrel to her temple and pulled the trigger, lowering her dead weight to slump across David's chest. Retrieving a washcloth from the bathroom, I used it to clear my prints from the gun before setting the scene accordingly.

Jasmine's fingers were taken from the knife and the gun placed into the lifeless grip of her right hand. I knew well the significance of "powder burns" on a shooter's hand and how the absence of such with Jasmine would undermine the scene. With that, I guided her hand and fired a round into David's head, positioning her hand to where it would be if it were indeed a murder/suicide. I left immediately after, using the washcloth to wipe down behind me.

HIV steals a person's sanity and transforms the individual. I evaluate Jasmine's behavior, as well as my own, and know this to be true. Jasmine had been merciless, if not savage in her killing of David, and I had executed the girl without a moment's hesitation. I understand my satisfaction at David's death, but Jasmine was innocent. She was a victim like me, yet I'd killed her as if she'd been nothing more than a fly on the wall.

That alone is credence to my assessment. In no way am I bothered by it; I'm merely acknowledging the truth. My diagnosis, however, is something else altogether. I am truly devastated by it. I feel all alone and isolated, and I honestly don't know what to do.

DEAR DIARY,

After documenting my encounter with Jasmine and David, I withdrew within, taking off from work and confining myself to my home for over a week. It is hard swallowing the fact I'm fated to die. It's something that neither taste good nor goes down well. It's even difficult to digest; more than a week has past and I sometimes vomit at the thought.

Several days ago, David's mother called with question regarding her son's whereabouts. I feigned concern and informed her of my last phone conversation with him and his promise to come over. My best friend, Kenya, rang my phone just after eleven the following night, excited and breathless.

"Hey, girl!" Kenya exclaimed. "Did you catch the news?"

I hadn't. In fact, I hadn't been watching any TV, so distraught was I with my diagnosis.

"David's dead, girl!" was her exclamation.

"No!" I fronted, though my mood was such that I couldn't get fully into it.

"Yeah, girl. His momma found his ass chained to his bed

all stabbed up with a bullet in his head. Mmm-hmm. Just what his cheating ass get."

"Slow down, girl. What are you talking about?"

"I knew he was no good. Some bitch he was fucking went crazy. Stabbed him up and shot him in the head. Then she killed herself right on top of him."

My diagnosis preoccupied the whole of my mind, and I hadn't much considered myself a suspect in their deaths. However, it was nice to know everything had gone as planned and the Authorities wouldn't come my way. Even so, I seriously wasn't up for conversation and quickly concluded the call, claiming the need for solitude and time to sort things out. After all, cheater or not, he had been my boyfriend. I didn't even attend his funeral, knowing well my behavior would be justified. I cared nothing about his death and realized neither did I care about anyone else's.

I'm HIV positive and fated to die– and I want others to die as well. These were my thoughts a few days ago. I have since embraced them and have made the most spiteful decision a human being can make; I will commence to build a Circle of Death, and the pages to follow will portray the process.

DEAR DIARY,

    I work at La Sway, a mid-class restaurant/bar. There is always a stream of hungry men passing through; therefore, it is a ripe spot for recruits. A male group of four entered around noon, and I immediately set upon them, sliding over to the hostess and urging her to seat them in my section. They were all nice in the area of appearance, but that didn't matter, only my intent and the end result.

    Once they were seated, I became the sweet, charming, and seductive server, standing close enough to brush my leg against the one who sat closest to me. I served their orders and lingered at their table, chatting away. Subtle passes were made and conversation became implicitly sexual. They expected me to choose, but I made a point of speaking to each in turn, leaving the impression I was "down for whatever." With their bill I also left my number, and I am certain at least one of them will call.

DEAR DIARY,

I got a call from one of the four guys. His name is Joe. He said he likes my personality and wants to kick it with me to sample more. And women fall for this? I'm sure it's more than my personality he wants to sample. His conversation was fundamentally boring and transparent, so to speak. He asked questions like: How old am I (which I thought rude)? Am I currently involved with anyone? Do I smoke or drink? Can I cook? What do I sleep in?

Though he spoke those words, the underlying questions were something else entirely. He was really asking: How mature am I? What could he do to relate to me? What obstacle must he bypass in order to have me? Could he use alcohol or drugs to influence my decision to fuck? Would it all go down at my place or would there have to be other arrangements? Would I cook for him? What would he have to peel off if he woke in the night and wanted more of me? Of course I played his game, and my answers were something like: Twenty-four; Not involved; I live alone; I can cook; I sleep naked.

I agreed to hook up with him tomorrow after work. Due to the nature of this mission, I wouldn't give him my home address. If we were to go out, I told him, I'd take my own car and we'd have to meet somewhere. He claimed to understand my caution, and we settled on a time and place, though he wouldn't say what he has in mind. Whatever the case, it will definitely end with him trying for sex. To that, of course, I'll offer no resistance. In fact, I'll do my best to encourage him…

DEAR DIARY,

Joe was brought into my Circle, tonight. The rendezvous was at McDonald's on Waters Ave. and Eisenhower Dr. I arrived just after 9 p.m., and he pulled in shortly after, providing the option of a movie or a little something to eat and drink from Capone's, a sports bar at Eisenhower Square. I chose the latter, where we played pool, drank daiquiris, and ate hot wings.

Afterwards, I followed him to his place, wasting no time getting at him the second the door was locked behind us. He turned to find me on my knees before him, undoing his pants to suck his dick. Startled, he said, "Damn, baby, it's like that?" I'm not so quick to take a dick in my mouth, but my aim was to trick him, to have him neglect the use of a condom.

Naked, in his bed, I straddled him, working my hips to smear my wetness to his stomach. It drove him wild. He encouraged me to take him, but I didn't. I wanted him to seal his own fate, to willingly step into the arms of Death. I rose, extending my invitation. Steady with his aim, he brought the head to rest against me, dead center; eager for me to impale myself upon the length of him. I refused here as well, and he responded the way I knew he would, gripping my waist, thrusting in and pulling me to.

I had only one purpose in fucking him, and in no way did I expect to find it physically pleasing. However, as I rode, I found myself enjoying it. There was something exciting in what I was doing to him. I moved faster, grinding my pelvis against his. Several times I rose to work the head before giving myself a pleasure-jolt in dropping down again. He, too, found this pleasurable, and begged me to repeat the motion. I got carried away, spinning around to ride backward, bending forward to offer the view of himself sliding in and out of me.

As my excitement grew, I rode him roughly, using the spring-mattress and the countering force of gravity to bounce on him. He encouraged me to spread my knees farther, so as to take him deeper. I complied, and he, in his want for more, double palmed my ass, adding his strength to the force of gravity. From there, it wasn't long before his toes curled and his grunts became groans. I hopped up just in time to watch him cum all over himself, his body racked with convulsions.

There was something erotic in seeing him shake like that. As he lay panting, I headed for the bathroom to clean up, gathering my things to leave thereafter. I drove home still picturing his shuddering convulsion, smiling, knowing he wouldn't find the tremors of Death so gratifying.

DEAR DIARY,

So far today hasn't gone well. Last night Kenya and I went out clubbing and I didn't get home 'til late. I woke this morning with a hangover, two hours late for work, and my boss fired me. It came as no surprise considering my recent weeklong absence. At least my bills are paid up for this month. If worse comes to worst, I can always move in with Kenya, though I'll have a time turning aside her advances. She likes both men and women. She's real pretty, but I'm not feeling that sort of thing. However, the loss of my job doesn't impede the expansion of my Circle. I'll just have to find new hunting grounds, which should be easy enough. Horny men are everywhere. I need only to- my phone's ringing...

The caller was some guy I don't remember from the club last night. Says his name is Tim. He thinks we should talk and get to know each other in a quieter environment. He asked me to have dinner with him later on tonight at Island Breeze. Why is it I "think" he wants to fuck?

DEAR DIARY,

Moments after my last entry, Tim called again. Something had come up, he said, and tonight wouldn't be a good time for us to get together. However, he did bring to my attention he would be free within the next hour and could then stop by, if I was okay with it. I'm almost positive nothing had actually come up; he was merely thirsty to fuck and couldn't wait. I too was thirsty, so I conceded.

The music pumping from a brown Grand Prix rattled my apartment windows, bringing me out the front door to investigate. It was Tim. He was setting fire to a blunt as I hopped in, that on which he pulled twice before handing it over to me and tossing the car in gear. He said we'll have lunch at Mantraster's, and we can do whatever afterwards, but he first had a few plays to catch.

We never made it to Mantraster's, and neither did he catch any plays. Moments away from my door, Chatham/Metro pulled us over. I attributed the stop to speeding or loud music, but later found it was neither. Panicked, I made to snuff out the blunt.

"Keep it burning," Tim instructed, pulling over to the curb. "And put on your seatbelt."

Scared as hell and not wanting to go to jail for a fucking blunt, I handed it over to him, silently questioning his intent. He took a hit, much to my surprise, as if he hadn't the least concern for the officer who, at that point, was exiting his vehicle and approaching ours. I just knew we were going to jail. The officer advanced and Tim held the blunt in hand, seemingly unconcerned with the fact. The smoke was visibly thick and to neutralize the effect, I switched the A/C controls to max.

The officer tapped the window. Tim ignored him, turning to me instead. "What happens next is going to scare the shit out of you," he said. "But I need for you not to scream. It will only break my concentration." With that, I was even more afraid, knowing not what to expect.

The officer tapped again on the glass, miming his command. The window was let down a few inches and smoke trailed out heavily. The officer stepped back, a hand coming up to ward off the airborne assault. "God damn!" he choked. "What the—"

Had I not been so afraid, I would have laughed. The officer regained his composure and approached the window a second time, instructing Tim to shut off the motor and step out of the vehicle. I mentally protested the fact the officer had forgone the request for license and registration; not that Tim would've been any more compliant with that. He mumbled something with what looked like a regretful shake of his head, taking another hit from the blunt. With no regard to the officer, he extended it in my direction and asked me to hold it. "Hell no, nigga," I told him. "Are you crazy?" Although I'd already drawn that conclusion. "You see that police right there. Nigga you better put that shit out." He shook his head, uttering something to the nature of it being way too late for that.

The officer, having called for backup, repeated his request for Tim to shut off the motor and step out. "That's out of the question," Tim said. The smoke lent arrogance to his demeanor. "But I'll tell you what." He paused and took another hit from the blunt, and I can't believe the nerve of this guy. "If you hurry up," he went on, "I'll let you get back to your car before I smash off. That way you won't be so far behind if you decide to give chase."

There was no sincerity in Tim's suggestion, for we were "smashing off" even as he completed the statement, and the officer, unaccustomed to disregard for his authority, was left open mouth as we sped away on squealing tires. I tracked him in the side view mirror. He made a quick dash for his cruiser and was obstructed by passing traffic. It was then I understood Tim's decision to pull off when he did was not spontaneity, but precise calculation. He had experience in this fleeing form the law, but that didn't alleviate fear.

The chase began on Victory Drive, somewhere between Waters Avenue and Ott Street. Victory is fairly busy during lunch hour, a factor which facilitated our lead. The way the car accelerated spoke well for under the hood. The right of way was ours for several blocks, and I kept my eyes glued to the mirror as we tore up the two-lane side of Victory, bobbing through slower traffic, ever increasing with our lead on the cruiser until Tim was forced to pause for Abercorn's steady cross traffic.

Lights flashing, siren blaring, the cruiser closed to within half a block before a break manifested and Tim punched through– a break absent at the cruiser's arrival. Tim was heavy on the accelerator; regaining what had been lost in the precious seconds it took for Abercorn's traffic to respect the officer's rite of passage.

Drayton, a north bound one-way, was Tim's first turn. An obvious last-minute decision, however, for I was suddenly thrown forward and caught a fraction of a second later by the seatbelt's locking correspondence to suspension stress as he jammed on the brakes and swung a hard right.

A glass-front office building sat on that very corner. With the turn taken that way, I surely thought we'd crash upon the curb and into the building itself. But his skills were true. The turn, though scary, was perfectly executed. He made a left on 41st, and it was here, racing up a residential block, his cellphone rang. With what I'd seen so far, him answering the call didn't surprise me at all. Amber dying, he thrust the blunt in my direction, and I accepted it then, pretending to be every bit as calm as he. Afraid but not so much as I had been, I brought the blunt back to life while silently praying for the chase to end.

We came to a jolting halt at the corner of 41st and Bull St. as Tim, slowing, decided against pulling out in front of a southbound Cadillac. Phone to his ear, he glanced in the rearview, looked left then right, and prompted the caller to identify themselves as he got down again on the accelerator. We leapt away from the stop sign, accelerative force pressing me to my seat, shifting my weight towards the door as he turned south on Bull. We narrowly missed a black charger exiting Popeye's parking lot before we fell in fast behind a Chevy Tahoe, drew in close to its bumper, then swerved to pass it and the Cadillac, returning to our rightful lane just after crossing Victory, barely avoiding a head-on with a northbound Buick.

He spoke on the phone throughout. The caller, I gathered from Tim's side of the conversation, was an earlier mentioned "play". The situation was conveyed to the caller with an apology and Tim promising to knock off a few hundred or throw in something extra to cover any losses.

I knew enough about this lifestyle to know Tim's proposal was more than fair and the caller should have been content, ending the call. Not so! Tim recounted, undoubtedly at the caller's behest, the scenario for which had drawn the cop. His claim that we'd driven by a parked cruiser with the blunt to my lips, had me close to a verbal objection. However, I had been in possession of the blunt at the time, and I hadn't been exercising the usual caution in "holding it down".

The call ended before our West turn on 60th. Here, again, we lost sight of the trailing officer who had put in a second appearance shortly after crossing Victory. The distance we had on him was so that the left on Boyd St. and the consecutive one on 61st went unobserved. What came across as random turns had been a tactful strategy of doubling back; we saw no evidence of the cruiser as we came again to Bull, turning North onto which and pushing the stretch to DeRenne Ave. Tim took 516 to the Southwest bypass, whisking us out of the neighborhood to the outskirt of Savannah.

Tim apologized for scaring me, congratulated me on

how well I'd handled the situation, then questioned my familiarity with such. He suggested we have lunch at a hotel and relax for a while. It didn't surprise me that he still wanted to fuck, so we ordered Denny's from our suite at La Quinta and had lunch there. I had French toast with eggs and sausage, while Tim settled for potatoes, pasta, steak, and broccoli. I sat on the bed across from his position at the table, my legs suggestively parted. He carried on a conversation that remained clear of sex, though he couldn't keep his eyes from between my legs. I became excited in being so close to giving him something that would someday bring about his demise.

The lust in his eyes was unmistakable and highly contagious. I remember hoping he'd be as skilled at sex as he was at driving. Excitement got the best of me and I sat my plate aside, leaning back on my elbows and parting my legs wide for him to see; a language clear as English. He abandoned his plate and came over to me, running a hand straight up my skirt. My panties were soaked.

"Fear is such a wonderful aphrodisiac," he said. He honestly believed that is what had turned me on when it was actually the idea of slipping him poison. He pulled down my panties and attempted to slide in before removing the rest of my clothes. I knew then that he wouldn't use a condom.

He had my legs in the air and his member out through the zipper. Just like that I could've let him plunge right in, but I didn't. Men can't handle this position with legs up, though they frequently ask for it. Something about the position makes them come quick, and this surely would have been the case if I would've let Tim get it that way.

With that, I planted my feet to the mattress and told him he had to do it right. This too was clear; he stripped me naked and stroked me over before sitting back to remove his own clothes. I feared for a second he'd be calm enough to think about protection. But when he covered my body with his I knew a condom was the last thing on his mind. The mode of sex he indulged was something close to lovemaking, and he wasn't bad at it. He hooked his arms behind my shoulders, grinding his hips to mine. By the way his member slid against me, I thought he was having trouble getting it in with no hands. Then I noticed the repetitive motion; the way it slid just between the folds and up against my clit. In this manner he brought me to climax. Although I tried, I couldn't hide it from him.

The tremors intensified and I was alone in motion. Tim had gone still somewhere along the line, leaving me to pleasure myself against him. I opened my eyes to find him staring down at me with the biggest of knowing smiles. I was conscious and embarrassed, but I couldn't stop; I kept grinding, milking every sensation.

"Powerful, wasn't it?" he questioned as my grinding subsided. I collapsed beneath him and could only nod and furiously blush. "Powerful" is definitely a word to describe that orgasm. It left me tingling; until now I've only read about it. He entered me, and I held him a second, softly moaning and savoring the moment of stealing him with Death. It felt wonderful.

As he pumped his life away, my excitement rose anew in contemplating the women he would later take to bed. I grew even more excited with the idea of them in turn taking others to bed, and so on; the ultimate Circle of Death. My level of ecstasy exploded! I clutched him tight, banging my pelvis to his like a sex starved mad woman.

He put my legs up, and I knew the end was near. He drilled savagely, putting his weight behind his every thrust. Some call it "dropping hella wood", but Tim was only average in size, so I wouldn't exactly say he was dropping hella anything. Even so, it felt hella good though.

Within those few minutes of furious pounding, I told him to "beat this pussy". Never once did I tell him to come in me, and I had to push him out to keep him from doing it! After he caught his breath, he tried for a second round. I was so pissed I refused to oblige him. He pleaded for me not to be upset, explaining how difficult it is for a man to simply stop right in the middle of it. I understood well, but I'd already given him Death and felt no desire to indulge him further. He got the message soon enough and lay down beside me, softly snoring in seconds.

As a woman, it feels good to fuck a man to sleep. In this matter I took even greater satisfaction in knowing this same fuck would someday bring him to a more permanent sleep. I lay there and waited for some sense of guilt but felt none.

I don't know how long I've been infected, but my awareness of the fact is fairly recent. After dealing with David and Jasmine, I didn't leave home for a week. Withdrawn, I moved dazedly about my apartment with the repetitive question of why. I lost weight in those first few days; the sense of devastation was overbearing, and I hardly ate. I was angry also and David's death did nothing to decimate that anger. It merely grew in my time of seclusion, a budding hatred for the world!

I know what I do to be heartless, cruel, and selfish in that I want others to suffer as I do, but I don't care. I should be appalled at my behavior, yet I'm ecstatic with lust for the next victim. In contemplating both my thoughts and desires, I have to question who or what I've become. I am certainly not the woman I once was; she would never even dream of what it is I do now to others.

DEAR DIARY,

It's been three days since the car chase and that "powerful" orgasm with Tim. Lately I've been stuck with a sense of depression. It may be due to the fact I'm fated to die early. The more I think about it, the more people I want to take with me. This is the worst thing for me since having to leave college.

Last night I cried for nearly an hour, but I can't say what brought the tears. I'm sure some part of me hates what I'm doing to people. Maybe it's the inner struggle of right and wrong that's causing my depression. I called my boss and pleaded for my job back, explaining how I'd had a serious case of Death in my life but was certainly able to handle the responsibility once accorded to me. I start again tomorrow and intend to have another victim as well. For now, I think I'll call Kenya and see if she'll come smoke with me. That should ease my mind a little

DEAR DIARY,

It's a little past ten p.m. and I'm still buzzing with excitement, the sensation I get from administering Death. Earlier today, while serving the last three men before my break, the trap was sprung! My feet were tired and I was agitated. In a tone which belied my irritation, I encouraged them to be quick in placing their order.

Equally polite, one of the three– all of them around my age– questioned my haste. I responded accordingly, and he suggested we spend half my break with him massaging my feet. I'm not so easily had, so naturally I'd refuse any such a suggestion, but now my purpose compels me to fall for almost any line thrown my way.

I looked them over and addressed the one accordingly, informing him of my hour-long break, asking what's to follow the half hour with my feet. A subtle exchange transpired between them before he stated the choice was mine. The three of them, he continued, were in town for a day or so, and I could spend my lunch hour with them in their suite at the Marriott, practically right next door to my job.

I pointed out his use of the words "them" and "their," which meant he no longer spoke of just him and me, but his friends also. I had no problem with that. In fact, I latched on to the prospect of poisoning three over one. So as not to appear suspicious, I played my part.

I made clear to their spokesman that I'd accompany him alone, asking only for a foot massage and a little "consideration" once my panties were off. But if his friends were to be included, he had to come with something other than a foot massage. Another guy spoke, asking quite frankly "how much exactly?" I looked them over, pretending to think before giving the price of three hundred.

The third guy spoke then, asking me to turn around so that he may see my ass. I complied, knowing he'd be more than happy with what he saw. The second guy asked was I "naturally animated." I had absolutely no idea what he meant by that! The first guy responded to my confusion, translating his friend's use of words. He wanted to know if I would "fuck back." I told him I would if there was reason to. He seemed satisfied enough with that.

They stood and the second guy dropped three one-hundred-dollar bills on the table, informing me they'd be waiting out front in a green Suburban. I clocked out, grabbed three condoms from my purse, and went out to meet them. We entered the Marriott by way of garage, taking the elevator to their fifth-floor suite. Excitement took me in the elevator. I pushed the first guy against the wall and slid my hands under his shirt.

In the room, the second guy took me by the hand and

led me away from the others. I wasted no time, telling him, once naked, to lie back on the bed. I knelt between his legs and made a show of tearing open the condom, strapping him up and positioning myself to ride. I moved slow at first then gradually picked up the pace, and in minutes I had him squeezing my hips and pulling me down, wanting to get deeper inside.

I did what I could to assist him in this, spreading my knees farther, arching my back, every bit as eager as he. I leaned forward, my face close to his and asked, "Am I animated enough for you?" His response was a passion-filled repetition of the word "yes." He grabbed a double handful of my ass, pulling me down ferociously.

I nearly lost the rhythm when his finger penetrated my ass. He'd given me the prep but I didn't recognize it, being that I've never had anyone bold enough to try this. The "prep" – him using my own moisture to lube my anus–doubled as question to proceed. Most people understood-some better than others- the silent language of sex where pleas, demands, questions, and desires were expressed as well as interpreted by one gesture or another.

The moment his finger intruded I knew I'd somehow given consent. Therefore, I couldn't be angry. Consent or none, though, the finger felt nice! The shock subsided and I found myself trying to ride both his dick and finger. The double penetration took me closer to climax. But he came before I did, and I felt cheated. I held my frustration and hoped the next man would do better.

Next came Aaron, the one who offered to massage my feet. I gave him a condom and watched with hungry anticipation as he strapped up. I lay there, legs drawn up and knees parted, dripping wet. I had a hold of his dick trying to shove it inside me before he even settled properly. He was larger in size, going deeper than his friend. This is it, I thought, but I couldn't have been more wrong. Two minutes into it, my passion on the rise, he stopped.

There was no climax; he simply quit stroking and stared down at me. Impatient to be on with it, I asked what the problem was. He went on to say he'd rather I played at being uninterested in the act. I couldn't believe it! A nice, hot and hard dick inside me, and he wanted me to be still. I've heard of men who preferred "dead pussy", but I've never encountered any– until today.

Being that my service was bought, I felt it only fair to oblige him, so I removed my arms from around him and lay as he asked. I thought it would be easy, just lying there, but it was everything but. In seconds I found myself moving again, going from subtle to obvious participation; my hands sliding along his back, pulling him closer, arching to meet his thrust, catching him dead center, loving every bit of it– and again he asked me to stop.

I'm skilled at sex, so his refusal to accept participation baffled the hell out of me. I couldn't help but wonder if he even knew an eager, experienced and responsive woman offered greater access to her depths, allowing him to reach points within that he otherwise could not. There's also, in the bargain, an increased level of friction.

I made several attempts with my offering, but he wouldn't accept. At some point he went from asking me to be still to instructing me to resist; to say "no", "stop", "please", and "don't", to squirm away with half-hearted attempts at escape. I didn't need instructions on how to resist, I was tempted to tell him. I wished only to resist his foolish request. But I was obligated to comply.

I told him to stop. I squirmed beneath him, pushing at his chest. His passion came to life then. In response to my pretense, he hooked his arms behind my shoulders to thwart my escape, pulling me closer as he drilled harder, forcing me to take what I pretended not to want. I fought harder, and he responded with even more aggression, which I found pleasurable. His breathing became heavy, so too did mine.

He made an attempt to put up my leg. I fought that as well, saying no. He overpowered me of course, pinning my knee to my chest, putting even more force behind his thrust. By then, I was so close to climax I could no longer pretend. I screamed. Not no, don't or stop, but words of consent and encouragement. I offered him my other leg, but he wouldn't take it. In fact, he released the one pinned, saying I was making things more difficult than it had to be.

I knew conflicting emotions, those of confusion, anger, and longing. In my life, I can't remember a single moment when I wanted to fuck someone who had me so upset. Again, I felt cheated, as if they were using me. With my eyes, I shot lasers up at him. Once more I went still, letting him have at me. My anger enabled me to lay there long enough for him to finish. Before leaving, he said he wanted me to understand that the money I'd received left him free of obligation. Had it been just the two of us, his request would've come after my point of gratification. Somehow that made me less angry, though it did nothing to lessen my desire. I needed to get off.

The third guy entered and took the last condom. He knelt between my legs and cupped my pussy, rubbing it, sliding his fingers between the lips. His hand came away wet. He examined the moisture, lifting it to his nose, and his erection grew right in front of me, further turning me on. He strapped on the rubber and fell hard between my thighs.

His entrance was jolting, in a pleasing sort of way. He was even bigger than the other two, and still I caught him. Surprised, he made his second thrust harder, testing, challenging. I caught it as well, though my gasp wasn't that of pure pleasure. Not quite satisfied, he thrust in a third time, giving more. I arched up for this one also, receiving a level of pain almost equal to that of pleasure.

I knew the next thrust was to be more powerful, possibly tipping the balance of pleasure. I knew this but didn't back down. He thrust; I caught it, knowing every thrust thereafter would come with equal force unless I pleaded out. The challenge had been taken on silently, and the plea would be in likewise fashion; reducing the ferocity of my thrust to him.

Of course I did no such thing. So, we fought with blows of ecstasy, his heavily laced with pain in his attempt to force submission upon me. He asked to get it from the back. I assumed the position quick, and again he set out to make his point, drilling me hard. From this position, I was expected to resist the backwards pull, to change the deep, access granting arch in my back to the more restricting hump; to try and run from the dick.

I did neither. I planted my knees wide, maintaining my arch, tossed back my head to add to it, and rammed my ass into his pelvis. Unwilling to accept my point, he took it a step further, placing a hand to the back of my neck and pushing my head down into the pillow. It altered his angle of penetration, going deeper still, leaning in to drop hella wood. Yes, "hella wood."

Even here, I gave no plea for mercy, which would've been in sliding to my stomach. This position brought about the conclusion of our silent confrontation; having established that he could be as rough as he wanted and it, in turn, would be accommodated. I did reach climax with him, and I fell to my stomach when it happened, screaming, trying to muffle my excitement in burying my face in the pillow. He had yet to catch his, so I kept my ass tooted up so as not to restrict access.

He fell over me, bracing his hands to either side. This also enabled him to make use of the springy mattress in rebounding me back to him after hammering me away. He collapsed on top of me, weak and exhausted, he asked can we do it again sometime; maybe after work, just him and me. I wanted to say no, being that all their condoms had holes in them and my mission complete. But somehow, I said yes.

At work and still buzzing with excitement, I wondered what made me agree when I'd already accomplished my goal of getting them with Death. A woman's moral view on sex is quite different from those of men. We can't, or won't, be as wild when it comes to it. We're more guarded, but that doesn't mean we desire it less. I'm crazy about sex, but it's been kept in check by that code, the standard women are expected to uphold. Somehow it's instilled within us that being loose about sex isn't proper, though to what degree varies with each woman.

My thoughts continued to run this line, and it came to me that once this hereditary condition is compromised, by whatever the circumstances may be– HIV in my case– a woman may become as indulgent as any man. The morality which governed my behavior has been broken, leaving me free to promiscuously indulge my sexuality, remorselessly destroying others in the process.

I am worn out now, fucking with Jason. He wanted me to stay the night, but I knew I wouldn't get to sleep if I'd done that. The blame, I'm sure, wouldn't have been all his.

DEAR DIARY,

Last night I gave Death to my mother's boyfriend while she lay confined to her bed with a broken hip, the injury which brought me there to begin with. On Tuesday, a city garbage truck ran through a traffic light and struck her Honda head on. I learned of this yesterday, when Aunt Rose called and asked if I'd stop by the pharmacy for my mother's prescription and run it over to her place. Rose was at work, my momma was in pain, and my mother's boyfriend wouldn't get in until later that night.

I felt sorry for her, which came as a surprise; I've felt all but compassion for the woman for more than two years now. I've yet to forgive her. The family had no clue as to our alienation. We, by mutual assent, have kept it between the two of us. It's a strain for us to be in the same room together. With that, I was of a mind to hand off the painkillers and be on my way.

She appeared happy to see me. I attributed that to the package I carried. We talked, and though the fact was never mentioned, she was hungry. Popeye's Chicken, her favorite, was just around the corner, but she knew better than to ask me to go for her. The answer would've been no, given in the form of an excuse she would have to respect.

Pills on an empty stomach were sure to have her sick. In taking them, she'd only trade one ill for another. It should have bothered me none, but it did, and I found myself in the kitchen fixing her a sandwich. I sort of warmed to the thought, for I took her the sandwich and proceeded to prepare for her a hot dinner of fried chicken, corn, mashed potatoes and gravy. I sat at her bedside as we ate and played at more conversation.

At some point, she broke off mid-sentence and apologized for what happened, for the incident which had placed the barrier between us. Her eyes were tear-filled as she begged my forgiveness. So were mine, as I conceded. We ate more pleasantly, thereafter, our hearts free of burden.

She'd long since drifted off to sleep, and I was loading the dishwasher when "Damn! That's nice" was whispered appreciatively behind me. I'd settled on staying the night and had already taken a shower and was in one of my mother's nightgowns. I recognized the voice. I didn't mind the compliment. Not even the suggestive tone, but he's my mother's boyfriend and any such from him is unacceptable.

I turned to give him a word or two on ethics, but my thoughts were suddenly consumed by the memory of me coming home to find my mother having sex with my boyfriend on the front room floor. There had been no serious love between Donnie and I, but the sight of him drilling my momma– and by God he was drilling! Her knees were damn near pinned to the floor! It crushed me. Even then I understood that men were potentially, if not already, dogs. In that instant I learned women were, too.

I know how some men get off on the thought of fucking both mother and daughter. Knowing such, my anger was at her, not him. It cut deep to see such betrayal. The term bitch took on new meaning for me that day. Neither of them tried to offer an explanation. Hell, what could they have said? I cried silently, packed my clothes, and moved in with Kenya. There, I saved up for a place of my own. Last night had been my first visit in almost two years, and as I turned to chastise her boyfriend, I felt those emotions surge anew. It was time for payback. After all, it was her act of betrayal that sat me in the hands of David. It felt right for her to share my fate.

Instead of an ethical reprimand, I asked Curtis, my mother's boyfriend, how true his interest was. He stared, then looked towards the wall in the direction of my mother's room, uncertain how to proceed. He feared entrapment. Bending at the dishwasher and tossing in the remaining dishes, I could feel his eyes burning through my night gown in their attempt to see all. I glanced at him over my shoulder. His eyes were glued. His bottom lip trembled. He caught my gaze then flicked his own toward the wall in my mother's direction. I started the dishwasher and covered the distance between us.

"She's asleep," I said, grabbing his dick and finding it hard.

Instinct brought his hands to my ass, while caution took them away. He made as if to pry my hand from his crotch. I tightened my grip and assured him there was no setup; that

I knew he wanted me– the evidence was in my hand. I squeezed his erection for emphasis and brush my lips to his.

"I know you want this pussy," I told him. "You back away now and you'll never have this opportunity again." I let go of him. He held his ground, licked his lips, and glanced once more at the wall. He pulled me close and kissed me fervently; the lustful lover.

I knew I had him then, knew he could not back out. He'd taken the final step across that sinister threshold where the door slams shut behind, prodding the victim on to unknown dangers ahead. Passion prodded him in this case. I had nothing on under the gown to obstruct his finger from sliding between my cheeks to finger my pussy. I parted my legs to assist, more excited by the second. We stood there kissing, pawing each other down. My gown came off and fell to the floor. So did his pants, shirt, and shoes.

"I want it the way you were the moment I walked in," he rasped in my ear. I thought of my mother, of her and Donnie scrambling before me to get themselves together, and suddenly I couldn't give it to him fast enough. I led him in the front room to where I laid belly-over the arm of her sofa, my face in the cushioned seat.

He slid in quick. Before I could settle properly, he was already pumping away, filling me deep and fucking me good. My excitement grew. I muffled my cries in the cushion, wishing he could fuck me as hard as I knew he'd like. Over and over I visualized my mother and Donnie. I grew angry and, therefore, more excited at the scheme of things, at what took place under her nose.

I came– not as hard as I could have, had there been no need for discretion– moaning loudly for him to "take it." He pushed my head in the cushion to silence me, which only enhanced the experience. He dropped his weight down and clutched me bear-hug fashion, locking my arms against my torso while delivering stiff pumps. He had that hunched-back pose, and I knew well what was happening. I twisted violently in an attempt to dislodge him before too late. He held tighter and continued with those hunch-back pumps. Climax took him and, inevitably, his hold weakened.

I turned on him, furious, rebuking his irresponsible behavior. I wished for Death to take him immediately, for him to fall dead right there on top of me. However, I did calm down once he admitted being sterile. I retrieved my gown from the kitchen and went to my old room and slept peacefully. However, I did spend several minutes contemplating my treacherous behavior; how I'd shed tears with the woman only to send Death to her bed shortly after. Not so forgiving, is it?

DEAR DIARY,

My bedside clock tells me it's a little past three a.m. I've just awakened from a distressingly frightening nightmare, and I fear going back to sleep right now. It began a normal dream– me standing on a beautiful beach. The sky was bright, with fluffy white clouds as far as the eye could see, the sand warm beneath my feet. In the distance, figures walked in my direction.

I couldn't quite make them out, but I got the impression they were people I knew. I set out to meet them and, as I drew closer, the figures manifested as dark shadows. I paused, stared, and right before me the shadows bled together to become a massive wall of darkness. I stood horrified.

The darkness had a conscious, a presence about itself. Not only that; while I stood there, frozen, it seemed aware of my fear and, by means I can't put to words, conveyed a sense of reassurance, that it posed no threat. With that came a sense of promise, of unimaginable pleasure. The darkness approached; the sense of promise stronger. Though it felt genuine, there was underlying malice, the hint of something unspeakably dangerous.

Once recognized, it grew on me, invoking a petrifying level of fear. Certainty emitted from the shadow, a sense that fear is unwarranted in the face of promise. I felt I would receive something of them both regardless. My fear was deeply rooted. No assurance could displace it.

I fled the darkness, but it kept pace with me, refusing to be outdistanced no matter how fast I ran. The sand became cold beneath my feet, a chill echoing that of the pursuing darkness. I ran faster, so did the darkness move. The beach became a wooded forest with me ducking low-hanging branches, dodging trunks and tearing through brush in my haste to escape.

The forest itself became dark, leaving me to feel my way sightless. I refused to slow, fearing the darkness would have me. Though I could no longer see it, I felt it behind me, its sense of promise and danger pressing in close… I woke kicking and terrified. Genuine promise with underlying malice? It's confusing, and it doesn't make sense, I think I'll have some ice-cream now. I have no intentions of going back to sleep…

DEAR DIARY,

Kenya threw a birthday party at her place for another girlfriend of hers, and I was invited. There were women only at first, those parading around in miniskirts, clinging dresses, tight pants, short shorts, low-cut tops, and other revealing wear. It drew the attention of men, and I think Kenya counted on this, for when a car full of young males pulled up with question, her smile was knowing as she welcomed the group. She also encouraged them to call a few of their friends, suggesting they bring weed and whatever else.

The implication was clear, and it wasn't long before there were a number of males, lots of dancing, clouds of smoke, and a good bit of fucking going on. By all standards, I'm attractive, so I found it strange that three females approached before the first male stepped my way with sexual interest.

I was having such a nice time, feeling my old self and enjoying the simple ways of life, I almost didn't bite. I'd forgotten my diagnosis of HIV, which is why he got polite but little conversation from me. I don't know what brought the sentiment, but I suddenly remembered my condition of Death.

The awareness brought a strong sense of hurt, jitters to my stomach, and boundless rage. There I was having a wonderful time– and suddenly I remember I have HIV. I wanted to scream aloud, to strike out at everything. Then I remember Donta, the guy beside me running his weak ass game. My anger simmered and with it came that all too familiar excitement.

In that moment I wasn't me; I'd become someone else entirely. In my rage, I wanted to poison everyone at the party. In looked around and wondered how many of them already had it, and how many were like me in spreading it so freely. I remember thinking that I once would have never even thought to do what I currently did. But I once wasn't HIV positive.

The day I returned from the clinic bearing the dreadful news, I withdrew within myself, emerging as someone else. I never really saw the change; I only knew there had been one– a really big one. At the party, in that fit of rage, I felt myself become this "someone else," this woman who wants to wreak havoc. It's startling to watch yourself undergo such a metamorphosis, especially when the person you once were wouldn't hurt a fly.

I turned to Donta, and at my predatory gaze, he smiled, assuming he'd finally gotten my attention. We talked while making our way to the house. In the front room, people danced while others watched. There was one girl in a dress giving a lap dance to a guy on the couch. I've seen this done before; I'm positive she was impaled through the zipper. If others knew, they didn't let on.

Donta followed me upstairs, and I opened Kenya's bedroom door to find her, Birthday-Girl, and some younger fellow engaged in a threesome. The guy had Birthday-Girl from behind while she in turn had her face between Kenya's thighs. As one, their heads turned at my intrusion. The guy didn't miss a stroke, and Kenya, obviously nearing climax, guided Birthday-Girl's head down again.

I'm not bisexual, but at that moment I envied Kenya the service she was getting. It's been some time since I've had such treatment− and never in that fashion. Transfixed, I watched the proceedings. The guy kept stroking, Birthday-Girl continued licking, and Kenya's moans rose to a wail with the coinciding tremors of climax, sliding away from Birthday-girl's hungry mouth.

Understanding the sensitivity of the clitoris at climax in only the way a woman could, Birthday-Girl refused to let her escape, latching onto Kenya's thighs, gluing her mouth to Kenya's crotch. Kenya gasped rapidly and redoubled her effort to break free, clamping her thighs around Birthday-Girl's face and pushing at the woman's forehead, yet Birthday-Girl held fast. Kenya's struggle subsided with the orgasm's passing, and only then did Birthday-Girl relinquish her hold.

Surely that was pussy-eating at its finest! I've never before witnessed anything like it! I was shamelessly turned on by it all. Only women have a true understanding of how sensitive the clitoris becomes during, and immediately after orgasm. In this stage, if climax is brought by way of clitoral stimulation, further contact is almost unbearable. It remains pleasurable, for sure, but with it comes a… electrifying shock. Though Kenya fought to escape, the sensations were immensely ecstatic, as Birthday-Girl knew it would be, pressing the issue.

During the session of flee-and-pursuit, the guy managed to maintain his own penetrating contact with Birthday-Girl. Surely the experience added to his own excitement, for he drilled her something fierce. I actually forgot I was the intruder in this until Kenya, having caught her breath, smiled at me and said, "Well?" My comprehension was undeniably acute. "Well?" was actually the question of whether I was willing to give it a shot, having seen firsthand a sample of what a woman had to offer. And to give me more to contemplate, she added, "And that's not the half of it."

Embarrassment chose that moment to make its appearance. I blushed furiously, turning to Donta, who looked at me as if he, too, understood Kenya's "Well?" and was curious to know my answer. No doubt, he'd been eager to join them. I took his hand and led him out, following Kenya's request to lock the door behind me.

Three couples occupied the guest room: One on the bed, two on the floor. We left them and ran to the bathroom where Donta nearly tore the buttons off my blouse trying to get me out of it. Naked, with full erection, he sat back on the stool and beckoned me to ride. At that point, I wanted to be fucked but I didn't stress it. With no condom, I straddled and impaled myself on the length of him.

I stared him in the eyes, smiling at the unfelt, deadly poison taking root. He smiled back, feeling only pleasure, and that made me laugh. He took my laughter for excitement, which it was, but not as he imagined. He administered his version of caress to my nipples and breast. I moaned and gave to him his first stroke; a long rise, a slow descent. He loved it. So did I, moaning blissfully, pulling his head to my breast, implicating my desire.

He took a nipple into his mouth. I gasped, flung back my head and gave him stroke two, three, and every one thereafter - long, slow, and steady. Though excited, he neither rushed nor prompted me to hasten the pace. He took it the way I gave it, running his hand along my back, gripping my ass. He tilted his head, seeking my lips, which I gave with reluctance at first, then eagerly at finding it pleasant.

His lips danced from mine to one breast, the other, and back again, all in time with my slow, pleasure inducing Death-stroke. His mouth was marvelous. I couldn't help but imagine it between my legs. I wanted to ask him for it, but I'd long since learned if they didn't go down on their accord, it wouldn't be worth it.

So, I rode and fantasized, and keeping that same slow rhythm, I came twice. Near my third, he asked was I currently in use of a contraceptive. Riding slow, I told him no. He timed it perfectly; his question, my answer, his immediate reply for me to get up. My response was instant, standing off him, and no sooner did he come all over. I had no idea he was close to climax, so calm he had been about it. Had I spoken otherwise in response to his question of contraceptive, he would've skeeted all off in me.

He cleaned himself, said thanks, and left me in the closet searching for a fresh towel and rag. The bathroom door opened then closed. I came out of the closet to a guy taking a leak with no idea I stood behind him.

"Have you ever thought of knocking?" I said to his back. He turned- and pissed all over the seat and floor. He corrected his aim with a haste I found amusing. "Seems like you're having trouble handling that thing," I teased. He flashed me an embarrassed smile that changed to one of challenge when he asked if I thought I could do better. I'm not sure what he expected, but his eyes registered surprise when I sat on the tub's side with legs spread wide. "Let's see," I told him.

From there I got my first glance at his dick and, for a second, dreaded seeing it hard. He stood before me, dick inches from my face. From his back pocket he extracted a Magnum. Watching him tear open that condom, I felt as if I was about to be cheated. My whole purpose in fucking was to steal him with Death; I could not manage that with him wearing a rubber. To have me is to have Death. There is no other way.

"Let me take care of that," I said, holding my hand out for the condom. He handed it over obligingly. With renewed excitement, I sucked him hard. I then placed the condom into my mouth and used my lips to roll it down the length of him, a method he'd only heard of, if that. "You wild ainit, shawty?" he said, rolling the condom the rest of the way on. I only smiled.

He dropped to his knees and entered me, seating himself deep. I flinched. He smiled knowingly as he pulled all but the head out and came in again, harder. I gasped sharply. He withdrew a second time, and before he could slide in again, I placed a hand to his hip, holding him back.

He seemed content with the restriction, but then he moved my hand away, telling me to take it like a big girl. Strangely, his words excited me, and for a time I did take it, moaning, crying out. Even so, it soon became more than I wanted to take. I clamped my thighs on him. But he wanted nothing short of full penetration at that point, palming my ass and pulling me, placing a hand at my knee and forcing open my legs.

Though he pulled me forward, I slid ever so slightly away, my ass hanging over the inside of the bathtub, sliding farther still. He followed, and before I knew it, we were both in the tub with him on top. Here, the angle of penetration was different. He couldn't get up in it the way he really wanted to, though he was no less vigorous in trying. The result was more pleasing than painful. I even went so far as to give him my leg to put up but refused when he asked for the other.

Here, also, is where the condom broke. A Magnum is not a condom that easily breaks, especially when there's lubrication, which in this case there was plenty. I'm proud to admit being responsible for the condom's breakage. For the record: protection is useless when the person you're using it with truly means harm. Giving me that condom and letting me suck his dick was a deadly mistake. While rolling it on, I also bit a nice little hole in the tip.

When it broke, he didn't stop. Not that it mattered; Death had long since crept through that bite-size hole. He became more vigorous, panting, groaning, and telling me that my pussy was good. I, too, felt the greater sensation of naked flesh, wrapping my legs around him. I didn't want to let go, even as he struggled to pull out, skeeting all over my stomach and chest.

I was close to climax and his withdrawal left me throbbing with need. Without bothering to wipe off, I turned over and tooted my ass up at him, begging him to come in for just a bit longer. He'd lost most of his erection, but he didn't refuse. He only said, while rubbing the head against me to get it up, "You wild shawty."

In seconds he was hard enough to penetrate, and like a hungry slut- which I really felt for begging the way I had- I pushed back to meet him, smacking my ass hard against his pelvis. He became solid, not to be handled so thoroughly. Gripping my waist, he thrust in while pulling me to. In this he received no assistance from me. In fact, I began inching away.

He sensed my flight and gripped tighter, drilling me harder. It was both painful and pleasurable. Even so, I still inched away. He inched also, talking to me, saying "Oh, don't run now! You asked for it, didn't you? This what you wanted, right?" All too soon, my hands were at the tub's back wall and I could inch no further. Though I didn't think it possible, he drilled harder.

My response to this was to go upright against the wall. He countered with a hand to my neck, pushing my head down in the tub. By then I'd broken a sweat and was screaming like a tortured animal, coming closer to climax. He continued to speak to me. "Uh-huh! Where you going now? Can't run no more, can you? Take this dick, shawty! Take it like a big girl!"

Locked in such a position, I had no choice but to take it. The position gave him greater access and he penetrated deeper than before. For all my cries of bloody murder, I never once hollered "Stop." The pleasure/ pain combination was excruciating. Climax lingered just out of reach; brought close by pleasure, pushed back by pain. So close it hovered, like low-hanging storm clouds growing darker, gathering strength but never losing its fury, yet you sensed its power, the promise of intensity.

The door opened and someone entered the bathroom. My partner didn't miss a beat. Though the shower was in direct sight of the door, I couldn't see who'd entered; my face was just inches away from the tub's bottom. "God, Girl!" reached my ears, and I recognized the shocked voice to be Kenya's. There came the sound of Kenya relieving herself, the flushing toilet, and nothing at all of her exit. I should've been turned off, or at least bothered by another's presence, but climax was close, as it had been for some time, and I wouldn't be distracted by someone watching.

Eyes closed, moaning loudly, I strained for it. And finally it came. Hard. Real hard. Every bit as powerful as it had hinted it would be. It wasn't just one, but a whole chain, three or four back-to-back. I could hardly tell where one left off and another began. The spasms were strong. Once it struck, I could no longer scream, such was the shock of it. In silence, I shook like an animal in the throes of death, while he continued to drill. My tremors had yet to subside when he himself neared climax and pulled out to spill his release over my ass and back. "Oh my God!" Kenya exclaimed. "He's like a fucking horse! No wonder..."

Staring up at the two of them with cum all over my chest, stomach, ass, and back, I felt like a slut. I screamed at both of them to get out. "Horse" scrambled out of the tub as if he feared I would suddenly decide to scream rape. Kenya held the door open for him. When he was gone, she said, "It's like that sometimes. Don't feel bad though. If you ever want to talk about it, I'm here."

She left me alone with that and I was suddenly reminded why she's my best friend. I wonder if we'd remain close if she knew my condition. It took me some time to regain enough strength to get to my feet. Even so, my legs were shaky. After my shower, I found Kenya and told her I was leaving.

Right now, I'm sitting in my bed. It's getting late and I have to get up for work in the morning. With this session documented, I'll close this off and fall into one hell of a sated sleep. I only hope I'm not sore in the morning. I haven't felt pain like that since the loss of my virginity…

DEAR DIARY,

Social networks and dating sites such as Facebook, Mocospace, and Dateline.com make for excellent hunting grounds. In the past weeks I have dated eight individuals. Never a fan of social sites, I learned quickly that nearly everyone there was out for sex and the majority was not subtle about it. Meco is one of those. He was the first, therefore, the most surprising. We met on the chat line, and having listened to his greeting I signaled a request to connect.

"You trying to hook-up?" were his first words to me. Of course hooking up had been my intent, but so startled was I with his approach, I did not immediately reply. It got to me how he had only heard my greeting and wanted to fuck. We exchanged cell numbers and swapped pictures before he called me direct. Getting up with me was the topic and was in the first sentence of the first paragraph. As a result, I was more than eager to have him learn that the getting is not in all ways good. Though occasionally done, it is not my habit to bring victims to my home, so I met up with him in Memorial Hospital parking lot, leaving my car and climbing into the passenger seat of his Eclipse.

He took the back way out, placing a hand to my thigh as he accelerated onto Harry Truman. His fingers slid into my waistline, and I sensed this was more to gauge my reaction than to cop a feel. Meco used his knee to steer, pulled out his dick, and began to masturbate. He was satisfactory in length, and it was clear he was not shy about whipping it out. It is not often I see a man perform in this manner, and I won't pretend I was not interested. I watched closely; sure, he would go all the way with himself. Then he stopped, asking me to give him head.

Men try women all kinds of ways, I was suddenly reminded. However, they could go no further than women allowed. It was a little past nine p.m. and his windows were tinted dark. We could easily get away with what he had suggested, so I complied. Nevertheless, his audacity had its effect and I could not give it to him fast enough. Considering how abrupt I had been with it, however, he had to have thought I had been record breaking in giving it up.

Turned on with giving head and the idea of getting him with Death, my thoughts were to fuck him right there behind the wheel. I had no experience with this. I knew only the physical probability. My jeans undone and down about my ankles, I told Meco what I had in mind, but he was skeptical.

"Hold it up and hold the wheel," I told him. "Leave the rest to me."

Then I drew my heels into the seat. My back to him, I scooted over the gear shift and into his lap, sinking down the length of him. We circled Truman south and north again, both me and the wheel a bit much for him. Tint obscured our behavior, but his swerving could have gotten us stopped. I rode faster and he drove slower, reducing our speed to the minimum, though his handling did not improve. Getting people with Death has an effect on me, of course, but the element of danger took this session beyond what it usually is for me. I guess Tim was right; fear is a wonderful aphrodisiac.

Bracing my hands to his seat, I did my thing. He adjusted the back rest to lay back and the shift afforded me an uninhibited descent. I bounced for joy and moved ever closer to bliss. Meco's grip on my thigh tightened and his groans escalated as he moved to my rhythm. I knew we would come together. It was not what I wanted, but there was nothing I could do to change it. Climax was near; I wanted it and could not break stride. He cried out as I did and I rode as long as I dared, rising off of him as he ejaculated, his juices splashing my labium. The interruption stole from me, yet I was not up for another ride. Having gotten off, there was nothing else.

Social network encounters, as I have come to call them, are concluded shortly after sex and neither participant pretends to give a fuck about what the other has going on in their life. He dropped me to my car and was off with nothing more than a brief thanks. Wham, bam, thank you ma'am truly defines that encounter. I adjusted quick to the no-talk-straight-sex attitude that is inherent in network encounters.

Having been so condition, the encounter with Carlos

was something of another surprise. Though clear we would end up naked together, he was reserved, his approach similar in nature to courtship. I first caught this when he insisted we talk over lunch− after I had left no question I was with getting straight to it. I caught it again when he asked about the meal. I responded with adjectives that implied I spoke of something other than the food in question. He cracked a smiled and nodded appreciatively.

"Sounds nice," he said. "I will have some if you don't mind."

I suggested we skip the meal in front of us and proceed on with the business, but he declined, stating he'd move at whatever pace I chose, but he would rather enjoy lunch with me. He sipped at a glass of coke, in which floated a dark cherry.

"Either way," he added, plucking the cherry from his glass, popping stem in all into his mouth. "You will love the experience."

What made him so certain, I wanted to know. Then he plucked the stem from between his lips and offered it to me neatly knotted. The implication was clear, and the prospect had me intrigued. I examined the stem closely. One has offered, I thought, and one so with the promise of skill. So accustomed I had become with the straightforward manner associated with network encounters, I flat out questioned what he implied.

"It has conditions," he said.

"You want the same, right?" I came back.

He nodded, and I further scrutinized the stem before letting him know I was game and would even do him first. I do not recall much of what transpired over lunch, so preoccupied was I with his proposition. We went to his place over in Madison Apartments where I held up my end of the bargain. He took his time when it was his turn, touching and kissing me all over while speaking to me in a manner I was not so familiar.

"I'm fixing to get this pussy," he said, climbing on top of me. "Let me taste that pussy, shawty." His face descended to within inches of mine. "You gone let me taste it?"

"If that's what you want," I told him.

"Is that what you want?" he asked.

"I want whatever you want."

"And if I wanted to fuck you in the ass?"

I did not hesitate. "That, too, if you want."

All implied, was done. He ate my pussy then had his dick in my ass from every which way for all of thirty minutes before I insisted he back out of there and get where he was supposed to be. I got the impression he preferred ass over pussy, that he was already where he felt he should be. Though anal can be pleasant, I wouldn't want to be the girl who regularly has his attention, for the fact I don't care that way for anal.

We concluded our business, and he was again hospitable. There were no further attempt at seduction, and neither was he ready for me to leave, but I went home eventually, showered and had myself some ice cream, content with my accomplishment.

I later discovered that I myself had been victimized, and such was a heavy dose of reality for me. I am heavy with sex now. As a result, my hygiene and cleanliness is in high order, yet I detected an odor that isn't naturally me.

Enhanced hygienic attention could not displace it. I was first bothered then alarmed when discharge was visible in my underwear.

I was immediately in my car and heading to the gynecologist at Irvin Health Clinic when I realized it would not be in my best interest to arrive there with a new STD. My file has me as HIV positive, and they would, at the least, question my partner's identity and delve into my sex life in the name of public health and safety. Nevertheless, I needed the problem taken care of. I was conscious of both hospital and clinic. With that, I drove to Pembroke and sought treatment there, paying the walk-in fee and falsifying all personal info.

Chlamydia and gonorrhea is what they treated me for. I left with a prescription and was told no sex for seven days. Advice to which I now adhere− with only three days remaining. I can't say from whom those STDs were contracted, but things of that nature happen when you have unprotected sex. Though I maliciously set out to victimize, someone had gotten me− again. Intentionally or unknowingly, it was a reminder that one should have sex responsibly. I consider the way I once was and what I once represented, and I know I can't keep fucking this way. It's dangerous even for me. There's a lot more than HIV out there; all of which I would rather be without. I have to slow down but I will never stop. In three days, I'm coming out to play.

DEAR DIARY,

Today, my day off, I thought to do some shopping at the mall. The Stagg Shop had this nice little skirt set I'd been looking at for about a month, and yesterday I saw it in the sales paper with 20% off. With the sale ending soon, I couldn't wait. So off to the mall I go.

Like most women, I go shopping for one thing and end up with a hell of a lot more; my next victim included. By the time I reached the Stagg Shop, my hands were filled with bags from Macy's, Belk's, and Foot Locker. The skirt was available in three colors. I was in the process of choosing between beige and jean blue when a voice behind me whispered for me to take the black.

I turned to find a handsome black man near my age who introduced himself as Kevin. He was the drug dealer/thug type, but I found his manner attractive. "Why Black?" I asked, suspecting his suggestion to be no more than a conversation starter, for him to have no real answer. He surprised me by admitting that both beige and jean-blue were prettier shades than the black. While all three would do justice to my figure, he said, black would accentuate the golden-brown color of my skin, providing a more stunning contrast. He finished by saying the black would definitely be an eye-catcher, and how he'd love to see me in it.

The appraisal wasn't lost on me, and neither was his underlying desire, though subtle it may have been. Seeing me in that outfit, he would also want to see me out of it. A few months ago, it would've been hard getting me out of anything, but I am easy now that I walk with Death. Had Kevin approached me in this same manner before my diagnosis– had I no boyfriend– I would've given him play, for he'd managed to assist, compliment, and convey his desire without being offensive in the least?

He appeared a nice person, respectful when it came to women. For that alone I was tempted to send him away without my number, which, in the end, he did get. From the moment I first made my decision to victimize others, I've never once hesitated in following through with it. So the reluctance I felt with Kevin was something I didn't– and still don't– understand.

We spoke for several moments, and I experienced the usual anticipatory excitement at what was to come. I also experienced guilt, a notion I shouldn't poison him; that he should be spared, but I can't say why. I found the whole ordeal confusing. In the end, I made my decision and he left with my number, promising to call later tonight. He'll ask to come over, no doubt, and I will permit that of course. Once here, he'll want to fuck, and I'll let him do that as well.

DEAR DIARY,

It is now ten past one a.m., and I am wide awake, covered in sweat, though I was asleep only minutes earlier. I had that nightmare again, the one where I'm chased along the beach and into the forest by a wall of darkness. As before, it conveyed a sense of promise as well as that of underlying malice.

The forest darkened, and I didn't wake. I continued to dream, continued to run. Through the trees I caught the impression of light. In that direction I ran. Behind me, unseen but felt, the darkness followed, relentless with its sense of promise and malice. Terrified, I pressed on, ignoring the branches that tore at my naked flesh.

The forest broke, cut through by a road stretching away in either direction. Across it, more forest just as dark. Having had my fill of vegetation, I took to the road, praying my unobstructed route would allow me to outdistance the darkness. It didn't, though I moved at a rate inhumanly possible. With each shoulder glance, the darkness seemed closer. This only served to heighten my fear.

I ran faster, the flanking forest a blur in passing, and still the pursuing shadow lost no ground. At my redoubled effort, the darkness conveyed a sense of perplexity; it couldn't grasp my reason for fleeing. It projected reassurance, calm, and a feeling that everything would be fine. Underlying it all was that ever present sense of malice. In no way was I the least assured.

In fact, the soothing attempt had the opposite effect. Panic accommodated my terror. I found myself crying, wanting desperately to escape. The road became a river which opened to a large body of water, no land in sight. For what seemed like hours, I swam, faster than the creatures of the sea, and the darkness remained, drawing closer. I woke wet enough to actually have been in water. I trembled for every bit of two minutes. I'm okay now, but in no way am I ready to sleep…

DEAR DIARY,

Today is truly not my day. After the nightmare, afraid to go back to sleep, I went for a walk during which I bumped into someone who mistook me for a prostitute. Surely I wasn't passing up an opportunity to victimize the unsuspecting, so I played the part.

I'd just finished walking a few laps around the neighborhood when a blue Explorer pulled alongside me. The passenger-side window slid down and the driver, a black man in his late thirties, asked if I was "working." I knew what he meant and was offended by the question. I nearly ran him the hell away before giving thought to opportunity. I hopped in and we discussed a price.

He kept looking me over and I knew he wanted me bad. For a "suckie-fuckie", I told him two-hundred fifty dollars. He said he had one hundred and wanted only to fuck. Of course I'd have fucked him for nothing at all, but I saw the thirst in his eyes and held firm at two hundred. He pulled into a convenient store to get more money from the ATM. I ran in to use the restroom.

It was there I spotted blood on the tissue and realized my period had come. Back in the truck, I told him of my discovery and asked him to drop me back by the park. He looked me over again with those hungry eyes and nodded. Shortly after, he pulled into a dark wooded area and killed the lights. What have I gotten myself into, were my first thoughts? I was scared as hell and nearly had a heart attack when he reached over and slapped me across the face.

I just knew I was going to die. Why else had he taken me there? Suddenly, he had his hand around my throat and a gun in my face, screaming at me. "You little bitch!" he said. "What kind of game you playing? You think you can just get in my truck with those tight little shorts, get me all worked up telling me how you'll fuck me this and fuck me that, and then you come up with some shitty ass excuse about your period and try to run off and leave me with a fucking hard-on! Give me fucking blue-balls!"

Like I mentioned earlier, it was dark, but not so that I couldn't see the murderous rage in his eyes. Frantically, I reached in my shorts and pulled the bloody tissue from my panties and held it up to him. He released my throat, took the tissue and examined it. When next he spoke, it was with considerably less anger, though he made clear he cared nothing for my period; he intended to have me still.

He thrust the money in my hand and told me to get undressed in the backseat. I tried to give it back, telling him I wasn't comfortable having sex while on my period, and that I wouldn't be able to perform on the level I had promised because of it. He snapped then, grabbing a fist full of my hair, slapping me across the face. Between slaps, he managed to get my clothes off. Of course I helped, praying the beating would stop once I was naked.

With the gun to my head, he commanded me to suck his dick, telling me if I even thought about biting, he'd blow my fucking brains out. I was so terrified, thinking he'd mistake the slightest scrape for an attempt to bite. Fear made the performance a piss poor one, and he quickly grew frustrated with me, hollering that I wasn't even doing a job worth fifty cents. In spite of the insult, I think he knew the case, but kept shouting anyway. When that failed to produce better results, the son of a bitch started pushing my head further down on him, choking me!

The sick bastard didn't even want to let me up to clear my throat! When he did, it was only a brief second before he forced me down again. Men often push too far receiving head. A woman's natural response and defense against it is to put her teeth in the way, causing the male to instantly hold back, unwilling to scrape himself. I never knew how powerful an instinct this was until forced to fight it.

Not only did I want to scrape him, I wanted to bite the mother fucker off! If he hadn't had that gun, I surely would've tried! But as it was, I was afraid, and though he tried to shove it all down my throat, I managed to keep myself from clamping down on him. Son of a bitch! A blessing it was when he got tired of head and wanted to fuck. When next he told me to get in the back seat, I said nothing more about my period, or anything of reluctance for sex under the circumstances. I simply got there and waited.

From the glove box he brought out a box of condoms,

crushing all my hopes of getting him with Death. I should've known he'd use protection if for no other reason than my period. I became angry at what he'd forced on me. The fact that he was going to get away scot-free made it worse. I thought furiously on how to get him not to use that condom, how to go about damaging it. Nervously, I chewed at my fingernails. By the time he had his clothes off and the condom on I still hadn't come up with anything.

He wanted to fuck me at gunpoint, but I begged him to put it away, adding with it a promise to make it worth every penny he'd given me. With that, he practically threw the thing under the seat. I felt better, having been afraid the thirsty son of a bitch would get carried away and accidentally pull the trigger. So, to make sure he left it out of sight, in spite of my disgust, I responded accordingly. In size, he wasn't even average. What was enough to choke fell short of a size I'd call pleasing. In no way did I let it show.

I held him close and made all the proper noises, careful not to overdo it. At some point, he slipped out. The second it happened, I knew how I was to overcome the barrier and get him with Death. I experienced my first tingle of excitement. I displayed a little more enthusiasm, moving so as to make him slip out again. Feigning eagerness to have him back, I reached down to grab him, quickly using the jagged edge of my bitten fingernail to snag at the condom's reservoir before guiding him back inside me. Though terrified he'd catch on and kill me, I did it twice more before deciding not to press my luck.

I knew the holes were enough to let Death through. Knowing this, I became wild beneath him, telling him to fuck me harder, knowing well the force would drive Death juice through the rubber, sealing his fate. To take it a step further, I misaligned my motion to his, shifting at angles, causing him to slide in with increased friction along my walls, placing a greater strain on his damaged protection. I grew breathless with the effort; squeezing tight, holding him close, throwing myself against him as hard as I could.

When finally the condom broke, I experienced a triumphant surge of excitement. With it came climax, taking me totally by surprise. Somewhere in the middle I moaned "Oh, God, this is so nice!" referring to my accomplishment. He agreed, but surely for reasons other than my own. Afterwards he handed me a box of wipes, which I accepted, grateful the bleeding was only light. Even though I smiled every time he looked in my direction, I felt disgusted at the sex he'd forced on me. I never let a man touch me while on my period. And to think I actually came doing it… uhgh!

I was dropped by the park and left to make my way home, contemplating the beating and how he'd forced his dick down my throat. There was satisfaction in knowing what he'd walked away with, having made a deadly mistake in not respecting my wishes. To have me is to have Death, remains true. So does the fact that protection is useless if one of the participants bears malice. Until recently I wondered why sex hadn't been this nice before. I now know it's not the sex that gets me off; it's the underlying malice.

DEAR DIARY,

Up until yesterday, three people were spared by the presence of my period. At work, some guy came in claiming to be the owner of a spa and massage parlor. My attitude while on my period can be really shitty sometimes, and so it was the day I served him. For some reason he wasn't offended by my lack of courtesy. He took it as an opportunity to toss his line. He managed to let me know of his business and offered a remedy for my "crabby attitude" and fatigue; a massage and a nice soak in a hot bubbling spa.

Because he was both owner and masseur, he could provide this service free of charge, with an added bottle of champagne. This offer was made the same morning I had the nightmare and had gone out for a walk to get picked up, beaten, and forced to have sex during my monthly cycle. The very same morning I never returned to sleep before going in to work sore and exhausted. I wanted nothing more than to accept the guy's generosity, knowing he'd share the spa with me and receive my hidden offer of

Death. But circumstances wouldn't have it happen. And to cut short his persistence, I told him I'd love to accept, but my current condition would only turn the water a nasty shade of red.

He frowned at that, picking at the remains of his lunch, the idea obviously having killed his appetite. I nearly laughed. He was the first spared. Later, on the way home, I caught a flat on Harry Truman. So, after having the scariest nightmare, beat half to death, a dick shoved down my throat, raped, a stressing day at work; my day continued to spiral. I wanted only to get home, shower, have some ice-cream, and go to bed. Almost every towing company I called offered a waiting period of nothing short of an hour. I had everything from jack to spare in my trunk, those of which were no good because I have no experience with either.

I sat there stewing; my father's a mechanic and I can't change a tire. I cried out my frustration. Not because of the flat, though it was the final straw which broke the mule's back. I cried for all I'd been through that day, for the secret I shared with no one, for the fact I was slowly dying from an incurable disease. It pressed heavily on me how miserably lonely I'd be for however long I had left to live. No matter how I sexed a person, true intimacy would never be a part of it- something I'm really beginning to crave. No matter how many people I took with me, I'd still die alone. This is what really had me so upset.

I was in the middle of "why me?" when I looked in my rearview; a SUV had stopped behind me and someone got out. I dried my eyes and got out to meet my savior, a white male around the age of forty. Not bad as far as looks. He had the flat off, spare on in less than ten minutes. While he worked, I expressed my gratitude continuously. Afterwards, reaching for my purse, I asked how much I owed. He tossed back his head and laughed shortly, not at all insulting.

"Fortunately," he said. "Money's no factor; of that I have plenty."

Again, I expressed my gratitude, how I wished there was something I could do to repay him. Taking the statement for more than it was, he gave me a once-over and glanced significantly at his SUV. "There is something…" he said.

Though I honestly hadn't meant for him to take it that way, once spoken, the idea was entertaining. In that moment, I hated myself. The man had come to my rescue and there I wanted to ruin his life with tainted sex, and it was only my period that prevented me from going through with it. He apologized at my silence, begging I forgive his misinterpretation. I assured him there was none, but what he sought would be extremely messy if he were to gain possession. He smiled, looked me over again and sent me on my way.

I found myself wondering what kind of person I'd become. What kind of person wanted to repay kindness with Death? Even though I wondered, I would've poisoned the hell out of him right in his expensive little SUV had the circumstances been right. And thus, victim number two was spared. The third guy made good his escape a few days after, the night Kenya and I went to Club Sensation, a nightclub in downtown Savannah. Almost everyone there is out for a night of fun and sex. It's like that with many clubs, but more so with this one.

Women even prostituted there in the place, and not only in VIP. Actual penetration took place under the cover of grinding lap dances and the like. There was surprisingly little violence. People called it the "Pleasure Club," and there were pleasure-seekers aplenty, one of whom had been persistently seeking such with me. I'd been hit on several times that night, and all had moved on once they realized I wasn't fair game. All except this one who, after buying me a drink, refused to buzz off.

He made it appear coincidently so, but he followed me around the club for half the night. Several times on the dance floor I turned to find him grinding my ass. I am nice looking, but by no means was I the "finest thing up in there." With that, his persistence was baffling. When nothing else seemed to work, I finally told him about my period. By then, sitting at the bar, I was so tempted to give him what he so relentlessly pursued– that and more– just to teach him "no" is better than "yes." I couldn't bring myself to do it; bloody sex just doesn't sit well with me.

His disappointment was rather strong, which puzzled me further. I asked why was he so bent on pushing my way when others were more than ready to accommodate. He frowned, taking a contemplative sip of his drink.

"I don't know," he said. "With you I get the impression of a prowling jungle cat. Beautiful and dangerous. You have this, uh, alluring yet forbidden aura about yourself– and you don't even seem to be aware of it." He took a sip from his drink. "Shit, shawty. I don't know where the fuck it comes from, but you seem dangerously exotic.

It intrigued me how he'd instinctively touched on the danger associated with me. We finished our drinks together and I sent him away with a word of advice, informing him his intuition was not something he should take lightly, that to perceive beauty and danger— or any such combination— he should focus on the danger and steer clear away.

"Myself especially," I said when he asked was I to be included. I contemplated his description and wondered what was so alluring about Death.

The fourth man had no such luck. He fell victim yesterday, two days after my night at Sensation. Shower fresh, my day off, I dropped by Kroger for a little grocery shopping. On the condom aisle, looking over the selection, I began noticing glances directed my way from the young, white fellow beside me. I thought he was working up the courage to speak to me. I waited, looking over the condoms. Once it became clear he wouldn't make the move, I took the initiative, catching one of his glances with the innocent question, "May I help you?"

He blushed furiously. Fumbling for words, he apologized for staring. He went on to explain how he'd never seen a woman shop for condoms. While men could only assume what pleases her, she in turn would simply know, therefore his interest was in my choice. His response took me by surprise; I was prepared for anything other than what he'd said. I sensed nothing calculative about his statement. He'd been caught off guard and had spoken the truth. It astounded me; one so young with consideration for women. His condom preference was Rough Rider-Studded and Lifestyle-Ribbed. They weren't bad choices, but neither were they the best.

I explained that while some women were really wet, others were not so, and even the heavy soaker will, at some point, experience a minor drought. For those occasions the ribbed condom wouldn't be such a good choice, requiring adequate moisture to maximize its potential. Otherwise, the ribs pulled at her in ways not so pleasant, and the male is none the wiser. Studded condoms are nice, but women want to feel the heat of a hot and naked dick, which is why I prefer the Trojan-Supra. I told him it was magic and disappeared during sex.

"Disappear?" He flinched as if physically struck. "Doesn't that, like defeats the purpose?"

His name is John, and I've failed to mention he is cute, almost girlishly so, with dark hair, grey-blue eyes, and pale skin. I laughed and assured him the condom didn't actually disappear but emulated a convincing enough sensation to where both parties will investigate. He read the box for confirmation to my claims. Finding none, he asked, "Are you putting me on?"

I told him no, and he read some more, informing me the condoms were made of polyurethane instead of latex. "Which," I told him, "Is what makes them disappear." He shook his head skeptically, and that's when I told him I had a few condoms in my purse if he'd like to try one before making a purchase.

Unaware I meant for him to try it with me, right there in Kroger, he said sure. I instructed him to meet me in the ladies' room in three minutes and turned quickly away.

"Hey, wait a minute!" he called. "You're kidding, right?"

I told him I wasn't. He gave question regarding "the

catch", and I assured him there was none, but if he found my claims to be true, the experience to his liking, he was to pay for his condoms as well as my own. He agreed.

I waited in the bathroom for nearly five minutes before he knocked. He was hesitant at first, fearing some prank. I handed him a damaged condom, removed my panties and lifted my dress. That close to trapping him with Death, I trembled with excitement. Pants at his ankles, condom rolled on, he sat me up on the sink, spread my legs and entered me slow. In a little, out, in a little further, and so on. Never mind the fact I was wet enough for him to slide completely in with his initial thrust. He performed remarkably well for one so young. There was none of the savage drilling or furious pounding you get from men once they have your legs wide open the way John had mine, though I would have offered no opposition had he chosen that route.

In and out he pushed, deeper with each thrust. For greater access, he pushed my legs farther apart, driving deep to fill me with everything he had, kicking up the pace a notch. He kept it steady for a time before short stroking me, pushing in barely more than the head. I felt deprived but said nothing. The seed of deprivation grew. I wanted the deeper penetration, and the longer he kept from it the more I wanted it. The need became a burning desire which rose to a feverish peak.

I thought he too felt the need and would soon plunge in, so I waited; panting, trembling, wanting, and clutching him tightly. I dug my nails in his back, making my desire known, demanding fulfillment.

"Be patient." He whispered in my ear. I tried and

couldn't; the need was great. A torturous feeling it was to have him slide in, stop short, and withdraw, leaving the inner most part of me untouched, unsated. Each stroke had me praying for deliverance.

Men have a compulsory need to drive in and hit bottom. The fact that John refrained from this hereditary behavior said much for his control. I found myself sliding to the very edge of the sink offering what he should have been eager to accept. He refused my offer, backing away, maintaining shallow penetration. I persisted, sliding forward and using my hands to anchor myself, expecting him to catch me up and support my weight. My intent was to entangle him within arms and legs, nullify the shallow penetration by forcing him all the way in.

He saw the trap for what it was and held back, refusing to take my weight, leaving me to re-settle onto the sink. Thereafter, I gave up the silent language to verbalize my demand. "Be patient." He told me a second time. Just as I opened my mouth to protest, he gave it to me. He drove in deep. With that stroke came shock, relief, instant gratification, and a scream loud enough to carry beyond the bathroom walls. And though it shouldn't have been possible, that one stroke brought me to climax, while the second, third, and fourth, just as deep, gave it dramatic intensity. I palmed his ass and pulled him to me with all my strength. For thirty seconds at least, his every stroke seemed to trigger the orgasm anew.

Along with that one stroke, shock, relief, instant gratification, and orgasm, came the thought that the little shit had finally stopped fucking around. Afterwards, my head clear of passion, I realized he hadn't been "fucking around," and my orgasm hadn't been a coincidental occurrence. It was the result of measured strokes, restraint, appropriate pace, and perfect timing; him choosing the right moment to give what he'd made me so eager to have. And to think I nearly ruined it! I felt true admiration for the guy. Many men grew old and died never knowing half of what John displayed in those twenty minutes.

I honestly envied the woman he had eyes for, knowing what he'd given me to be only a sample of a full night's session. I asked how much time he'd put into learning what he knew and got the surprise of a lifetime. He claimed to have started at age seven. The real surprise came with the revelation of his biological sister, five years his senior, having been the teacher, providing hands on experience.

According to John, it began one night when he'd come to his sister's bed for comfort, afraid of lightning and thunder. While she held him, he asked about her breast. What were they for, and could he touch them? Her response was so long in coming he thought she'd fallen asleep. She told him that kind of touching was inappropriate for sister and brother. It wouldn't be right for her to let him touch her that way. John had no concern for right and complained to her.

"Neither do I," was her response.

"Then why can't I touch them?" he countered.

Again, her response was long in coming. "Johnny," she spoke his name softly. "The moment you asked to touch my breast I actually had an impulse to let you do that and everything else your curiosity compelled you to do. I balked for the fact I'm old enough to know better. You're all I have left." Their biological parents were killed in a car accident. "I don't want things to be awkward, or to have you someday hate me once you're old enough to comprehend what I allowed you to do."

"I wouldn't hate you no matter what," he said, and asked again to touch her breast. She laughed and told him to go to sleep, that he'd someday find the conversation embarrassing.

He waited for her to fall asleep and, careful not to wake her, explored her body. Softly, he stroked her breast, squeezed her nipples, and rubbed her stomach. Curious still, driven by what had to be instinct, he went below her navel to slide his hand into her panties. He touched her there and was surprised to find her different from him. Where he was hard, she was furry, soft, warm, and moist. In time he zeroed in on her clitoris. She squirmed at his touch, and he paused, fearing he'd wake her.

With an even lighter touch, he continued stroking her clit, thinking it to be a smaller nipple, intrigued by the soft sighing noises she made in response—no matter how light his stroke. He ran circles over it, stroked this way and that until she cried out. Whereas he quickly withdrew, thinking he'd somehow gotten carried away and hurt her. She sat up, breathing heavy, and he, fearing his sister's wrath, hastily explained how he hadn't meant to hurt or wake her. She confessed to having been neither asleep nor hurt.

He puzzled this over and verbalized his confusion. She gave him a long lecture on what he'd done, her response to it, why it was wrong, and how he was to never again, under any circumstances, touch her in that manner. She asked if he understood. He said he did and immediately asked to play with her nipple again, telling her he liked the little noises she made whenever he touched it. She refused. He pleaded continuously, pointing out her admittance to having enjoyed it earlier.

"Ok! Ok!" She relented finally. "You can play with it. It's called a clitoris, and you must always be gentle with it." And so, he was taught.

Night after night he visited his sister's bed, eager to play with her clit. It wasn't long before she introduced him to penetration, letting him, for nights, follow instinct for long periods on end. Eventually, she began instructing him in this; his inability to climax provided hours of erection throughout the night. Once he gained puberty, she taught him to relax during intercourse, and not to instinctively "chase" or "reach" for climax.

At fourteen, he was perfecting everything she'd taught him. By then, she'd fallen in love with him, and welcomed no other to her bed. She dated others as precaution against scandal. Those of the ones who took her out rarely got her naked. Thus, she became known for being "stingy with the pussy". That is, to all except her Johnny. Of course none knew that. Men coveted her type—or what they thought her type to be—and vied for her hand in marriage. Fed up with possible suitors, she consulted Johnny and together they decided she would fall for the young lawyer with wealthy parents. The husband has no idea of the doings between sister and brother. He thinks nothing of his wife's protective behavior towards her brother. Johnny's presence was never questioned in the husband's absence.

The tale sickened me at first, but I found myself listening

to his recount with interest. By the time he finished, we were at the register paying for my groceries. Oh, and he did pay for my condoms. Yes, John shared a deep, but twisted relationship with his sister. What he didn't know was he'd soon share Death with her as well. And she, in turn, will share it with the husband, which all contributes to my ever-expanding Circle of Death...

DEAR DIARY,

Beyond doubt I am truly evil. I usually lure victims with myself as bait. My father is a mechanic at Jake's Auto. That being the case, I'm privy to discounts and was there for an oil change, perusing the pages of a Sister 2 Sister magazine when a black couple arrived to retrieve their car. Jake, the shop's owner, presented them with their bill and highlighted the service provided.

Jake sent for their vehicle, the couple seated themselves cattycorner to me, and I stole glances at the male. That they were a couple was evident in their conversation, and it was reaffirmed with the girl's public display of affection towards the man. Their intimacy was beyond sex, I could see. Where she was physical, he was attentive. Where their behavior shouted "new," their familiarity spoke much for the time they had invested.

The guy surveyed both male and female as each put in an appearance, but no more than was appropriate, for she commanded his attention for the most part. I sought his eye, but he wouldn't bite. It struck a nerve and had me even more determined. He saw me checking him out, gave a nearly imperceptible shake of his head, then pulled the woman close for a quick kiss on the lips. The statement was clear; he had eyes for her only. Though he'd shown nothing other than respect for his girl, I was pissed—and jealous, so to speak. The girl was attractive, but she had nothing on me, which spoke more of their bond's purity. They reminded me of what I will never have, and I hated them both for that. I wanted to add something sour to all their sweetness.

Their vehicle, a green Honda, was brought around and presented to them. The young woman kissed her companion and was off, leaving him to take the bill— that which was done with an American Express—before he too was off in his Escalade. What I did next can only be described as stalking.

'Prowling jungle cat', a man once called me. I think it's cute, and I do feel predatory when I set out to victimize. I was angry, though I had no right to be when the two had only tended their business, and the young man had acted accordingly to my advance.

His name is Christopher Wright, and he is into PC repair, having opened a home-based practice complete with company cards. One of which he had used to cover the bill at the shop, allowing Tammy— Jake's secretarial accountant— to slip me the info. As my car was serviced, I devised a strategy, going over to Kenya's place thereafter, practically demanding she hand over her laptop. She protested at first, but that's my girl—she wants that literally—and there isn't much she would not do for me.

Besides, once I mentioned I'd have a specialist look at it, she was more than ready to part with it for a while.

I went out with the laptop to Kelp's Landings, at Christopher's home and place of business. The office hours were from 7 a.m. to 4 p.m. and my arrival was timed at closing. That the house had underwent significant renovation was clear. The east entrance, with its double doors, was commercially constructed, while the north face was residentially finished. The contrast was interesting, and I am not even into architect. Even an inexperienced eye could see money had been put into play. Inside, the two were intergraded. Christopher sat behind a desk from which he rose and rounded quick at my entrance.

"What the fuck?" he said, and I am inclined to believe he hadn't intended for those words to escape, for no sooner were they spoken than did his manner became professional. He wasn't for a second convinced I had come for repairs, though Kenya's laptop was clutched to my breast. He was correct, of course, and I didn't pretend otherwise. I spoke my reason for being there; omitting the fact I came with Death. He was clearly uncomfortable with my approach and all set against my proposal, proclaiming his love for Janine and firmly asserting he would allow nothing to come between them, that his world could not accommodate an affair. I let him carry on and he eventually addressed my audacity, having been caught off guard by it and the idea women would go so far.

"I've seen men go further," I told him, and he sounded the typical male in proclaiming a man's right to do so. "And women can't?" I shot back. If men were superior, I brought to his attention, how are inferior women to resist the very urges men could not? He was silent at this, having no words with which to counter. In front of his desk, I closed to within inches of him. "If you knew a woman's heart," I said, "you would think several times over before marrying your little princess. I cut the distance between us in half and was practically speaking into his mouth. "No affair, no drama, no hurting your finance; just sex.

"No strings attached?" he said.

"That's right."

"As in, we do it right here, you walk out, and you never come back?"

"Just like that," I said, close enough now to run my tongue across his lips if I were so inclined. He fell back, rather dramatically, as if he suddenly felt I would feel so.

"And Janine put you up to this?" he said.

I assured him that I had never seen him nor Janine before today at the shop.

"How much did she pay you?" he insisted, and I again stated my claim "Then why are you here?" he pressed.

I went into a quick narrative regarding women, their desires, and how more times than not they would slip their hands into the cookie jar if they were certain they wouldn't get caught. The dialogue, I am sure, will have him with nightmares, but nightmares are the least of his problems.

Covering the distance, he had put between us, I said, "tell me you don't like what you see in front of you. Tell me you don't want to know what it hit like." Females neither spoke nor acted this way. That he was surprised was apparent.

"No strings?" he said. "No trouble? No stalking? You

leave when we're done, never to return?"

I handed over the laptop with the explanation of having a friend who expected upgrades. His humor surfaced then, and I glimpsed what may have captured Janine's heart as he teasingly accused me of trying to get a freebie, arguing there were strings after all.

"The laptop adds legitimacy to my presence," I told him, "And all bases are covered if ever there were questions." He insisted I pay, and I agreed to pay only five percent and to provide a condom.

"One?" he complained, insisting I be fair, assuring me the laptop would have a worthy maintenance and he would be thorough with me, but he wanted at least two condoms. The laptop was placed atop his desk, and I was led to one of two reception couches. My intent had been to go in and do him quick, but I was feeling him enough to ride out if that's what he wanted.

"How long do we have?" I asked.

"Two hours," he said, instructing me to wait near the couch. There were a set of double doors through which he disappeared and returned shortly with a sheet, draping it over the couch and tucking it along the crevices. He was something nice out of his button-up and slacks, and I got physical, seriously groping him as the clothes fell away and he descended upon me. Having provided him with two damaged condoms, my excitement heightened with intercourse.

"I think," he said, "by the way you came up in here; I might know what you like."

There was a pause, him between my thighs, me savoring the moment, our gazes locked. Before I could question, he withdrew and situated me so that my knees were on the floor with him behind me and my head in the couch's seat. I got the point, and he was right of course; I can handle it rough. I suspected his aim was not primarily to please me, but to sate his own preference, that which I sensed would not fly so well with Janine. Or maybe he felt good girls− for he could think no less of Janine− should not be so handled or would not take well to it. I, obviously, wasn't categorized as such.

Christopher sent deep vibrations through my center in hitting me from the back. He was forceful but not overly aggressive. The hand to my head and neck was just so. He was also passionate, howling out and calling me names, "bitch" and "slut" being primary. I made no complaint and took no offense. I understand sex and what gets people off. This did it for him. For me, it was getting him with Death. I visualized the way he had earlier shaken off my advance, proclaiming his loyalty to Janine with a kiss. It set orgasmic fire to my senses as I contemplated my treachery, how my gift would tear their happy little world apart; my success. I screamed out my release, and he kept pounding. The condom broke and he did not stop. Conscious he may come inside me, I attempted to buck out the position, but was met with brute strength. My head was shoved down again and I was gripped tight at the waist. It set me to panic, but then he spoke, knowing my apprehension and conveying to me his desperation.

"I got it baby!" he said. "Don't fuck this up for me."

I considered what he had going for himself and felt he would not jeopardize it further by mishandling the situation.

I ceased to struggle, and the force by which I had been held was less menacing. The session intensified and I peaked with him, his pounding having come to jarring ferocity. He pulled out, then came his hot stickiness splashing to my shoulders. It spoke volume for his flame.

Christopher cleaned me up, rolled on the second condom, and we were at it again in multiple positions all over the couch. The condom broke and he didn't stop. Neither did I fight nor panic. He had proven himself the first round, and I trusted him to do so again. Most men do not care to pull out, I understand. It is an impossible feat for some, but Chris handled it well, cleaning us off a second time and requesting a third round. Though climax for him was rapid, his game was impressive. I consented and we didn't even bother with a third condom.

We concluded our business to lie panting, entangled on the couch. He smiled blissfully at me, and then guilt stole upon his features. I nearly laughed, wondering if his bitch ass may have realized how reckless he had been and what possible consequences. I told him not to worry, that I would hold to my end and there would be no trouble.

I thought Janine was a flawless companion to Chris, but I knew otherwise the moment he came; he skeeted all over my back and shoulders, apologizing for getting it all in my hair, claiming to never have shot so for before. Yes, Janine is pretty, perhaps all loving and faithful. Chris loved her dearly, but she didn't set fire to their bed. He doesn't come as hard nor skeet as far with her. Of this I'm certain, for he was extremely apologetic about the "unprecedented event". Janine will someday know her flaw, Chris' infidelity, and the consequence thereof. With that, I wonder if she will punish him for it. I wonder if she will know hate for others as I sometimes do. She is a good girl, from what I gathered, just as I had been, but I have become the definition of evil.

DEAR DIARY,

I got a call from Kevin today; the guy from the mall who suggested the black skirt. It surprised me to hear from him. Turns out he thought I'd given him a phony number. Said he'd sensed indecisiveness heavily that day, which lead him to believe I'd shot him a dummy. I remember clearly our conversation; what he called "indecisive" was actually me having trouble deciding whether to trap him with Death. My feelings were mixed. That in itself puzzled me. So, yeah, I can see how he got "indecisive" from that encounter.

He was pleased to have found my number correct. His interest in me also seemed genuine, but I knew better and waited for the conversation to turn sexual. He probed my background, curious as to my interest. At one point, he asked if I'd found an occasion on which to wear the skirt, again expressing his desire to see me in it. From there, I thought the conversation would go sexual. It didn't. He swung back to more mundane questions, bringing the call to an end after questions regarding my next day off, whether I had any plans, and whether it would be okay if he scheduled something for the two of us.

I admit to being surprised that the conversation hadn't gone sexual. I expected him to be subtle, if not outright, if only to gauge my reaction. Whatever he plans, however, I'm certain sex will be a part of it.

DEAR DIARY,

Kevin arrived around one, shortly after my shower, prompting me to answer the door in a towel. He was early and didn't seem to mind the wait, talking to me long distance from the front room with not so much as a suggestive offer to lotion my back. However, he did suggest my attire be suitable for the setting of a nice restaurant.

The restaurant turned out to be a Japanese one on Tybee Island, whereas he ordered for the both of us. I was served chopped vegetables, rice and chunks of meat, which I found delicious. Throughout dinner, he continued his game of getting to know me when, in all honesty, he only wanted to know what the pussy felt like. Thirsty to have him know, I fed right into it.

Afterwards, he tipped the server generously and led me toward the ocean to Tybee's great pier which, at one end, supported a concession stand. We were leaving the sand and climbing the planks when he informed me dessert would be one of my favorite treats. "And what's that?" I was curious, for we'd yet to cover the subject of favorite treats.

We made the landing and he swept his hand in a grand gesture towards a window serving ice cream, surprising me with his accurate assessment.

I got another surprise while at the window, when he named my favorite flavor— butter pecan— and suggested I try something different. A flavor, he said, that was sure to become another of my favorites. He ordered us a double scoop of Moo-llenium Crunch, going so far as to naming my cone of preference. Shoulder to shoulder, we walked the length of the pier, out over the Atlantic, and I felt more comfortable with him, more open to his probing.

As if sensing the change, he spoke a little about himself, proving me correct in labeling him a drug dealer. Though young, my age exactly, his character seemed more befitting to one much older. He's really practical, having no delusion about his drug dealing lifestyle, stating if he weren't "offed" or incarcerated, he intends to open some sort of business; a deli or something of that nature. To make it possible, he uses drug money to pay back small, high interest loans, forging a credit foundation that financial lenders wouldn't hesitate to build upon.

He sought a correspondence college to better his chances of success, aiming for a degree in business management. Kevin admits to being lazy when it comes to work, which is why he enjoys the flexible schedule of drug dealing, which enables him to do pretty much whatever, whenever, requiring almost no real work at all. He knew the err of his ways, and yet he accepted them for what they were, or where they could land him as a result. He regrets only that his occupation pushes women away. There aren't many who'd run the risk of building anything with someone who does what he does for a living. There were, of course, the gold diggers and hood-rats, those who thought the status attractive.

We lost track of time talking, looking out over the water, gentle breeze caressing our skin long after our ice cream was gone. I must say Moo-llenium Crunch is the bomb; vanilla flavored ice cream containing chunks of chocolate, caramel, walnuts, pecans, and almonds. I began to feel as if he probably did want to know me. The thought was nice.

We were back in front of my apartment when I realized the thought of poisoning him had been absent from the moment we first walked the pier. The fact I'm HIV positive was also gone from my conscious mind. The two struck suddenly, bringing a brief wave of depression, followed by the usual anticipatory excitement I get from what was to come− only not as strong. I felt reluctant. Close to what I felt the day we met. I shook it off.

He walked me to my door and kissed me good-bye. A deep, sexual kiss. I liked it. When I asked if he wanted to come inside, he smiled and shook his head, saying he had a few runs to make. "I thought you said your schedule was flexible," I challenged. His smile broadened. He gave me a once-over with lingering eyes at my cleavage.

"It is," he said at last. "But this is something I really need to take care of." He kissed me again and left, leaving me with mixed feelings of relief. Even now, I don't understand what I found so relieving about him refusing my offer of sex when my whole purpose is to fuck him to Death. I should be disappointed in letting him escape, but he'll be back; his dick was hard against me with that last kiss. It's still baffling to see him turn away like that, though.

I think he may not want it so easily attained, handed to him so directly. After all, he did so much as admit being sought. I'm of a mind to say he would rather seduce than be seduced. If that's the case, I can surely play that game. Some time ago, however, it wouldn't have been a game; he would've actually had trouble getting me to fuck. Regardless of who seduces whom, I'll be the victor. He'll reap Death as reward.

DEAR DIARY,

    Kevin called around 9 o' clock this morning, waking me from a dreamless sleep. He told me to get dressed− he wanted to see me and would do so over breakfast. "Nothing fancy," he said. "I'll be there in thirty." He hung up and I scrambled out of bed. And just as I figured, he arrived early.

    Mom and Nikki's is where he took me, a hood restaurant with home-style cooking. Nikki and Momma both greeted him warmly, addressing him by name, stressing the fact they've seen less of him of late. One would assume they were related if not for the sidelong glances Nikki threw his way. I expected laser glances from her, but she smiled and winked knowingly. I took an instant liking to her, and prayed she never got a hold to Kevin in the future.

    I ordered grits, eggs, and smoked sausage, while Kevin had smothered shrimp and gravy over grits with salmon (a combination I've never heard of), sausage patties, and bacon. Though "nothing fancy," the atmosphere was nice and so was the food, for that matter. The seasoning was just so I didn't have to add any. Putting me in the mind of an aunt's cooking.

Kevin has already proven to be observant as well as attentive, never losing my eyes for someone else's; a near impossible feat for men. Today, he added humor to the list with the way he cast at a subject and drew forth laughter where none should've been. He caught my frown at his plate. At which point, he speared a shrimp and held it out to me. I refused instinctively, but eyeing him intently, I came forward and took his offering, suggestively licking my lips and moaning at the taste.

He cocked an eyebrow then fed me several more mouthfuls, asking "How is it?"

"That'll be the one question I'd put to you," I said, my gaze meaningful.

"Is that so?" He sat down his fork, reached to my plate for the sausage and held it before my face challengingly. I took it seductively slow. I expected him to take me home and sample my implication. No such luck. He walked me to my door and made no attempt to enter. He kissed me good-bye and promised to see me later tonight if I'm okay with it. I ought to feel disappointed that he didn't take the bait. I'm not. He says he has business to handle, but surely he'll want that sample when he comes back tonight... I wonder if he'll even try to wear a condom...

DEAR DIARY,

This Diary is supposed to be a document of my Circle of Death. A notation of the people who have fallen victim to my virus. As of late, I've done nothing to expand the Circle. I'm sure those of the ones already infected continues the job for me. It's not as if victims are hard to come by; I get hit on a daily basis. Truth is, right now I have eyes for Kevin only. Not that I need have eyes to victimize.

We've been seeing a lot of each other lately, and I find him much to my liking. He comes over to cook for me occasionally, sometimes taking me out on my days off. I laughed the first time he offered to cook me dinner. He normally ate out, which gave me the impression he couldn't cook, and the thought of him trying was humorous. He arrived at my doorstep with an armful of groceries, and I laughed even harder thinking it had to be a joke.

Kevin appeared un-phased by my humor. In fact, he wore a little smile of his own. Preferring to work alone, he made me promise to stay out of the kitchen until he finished. I teased that he didn't want me to see how he'd burn shit up, but I'd still detect disaster by way of smell. I've never had a man cook for me before, and the gesture... made me feel special. He even turned off the lights and lit candles, bringing out a bottle of champagne. I just knew he'd fuck afterwards. He didn't.

Being with Kevin is exciting. I love his response to me. With him, I consciously forget I'm fated to die an early death. In so, I experience periods of happiness. I want him around constantly, and thirst for his presence in his absence. I know myself to be seriously attracted to him. He may be heavily attracted to me as well. Sometimes, at night, he calls me to come surf the city. These are times he's high on weed.

Music turned up, he would speed through the streets, head bobbing; at times swerving left to right. In this, no turns were normal. They were made to be... a little fancy. He'd swing in close to the curb, then swerve away before cutting the wheel back to make the turn, accelerating even as the wheel centers out. Gravity plays a part as well, shifting us this way and that, which is, after all, the desired effect. At least that's my interpretation of it, anyway.

He has this way of pumping the brake just before traveling through an intersection, causing the car to dip on its suspension, to bounce up at the approximate time of crossing, which contributes heavily to a sensational feel of lift-off. Cresting the rise, the vehicle bounces on its suspensions with Kevin bouncing to the motion as well, head bobbing rapidly. Lift-off brought the free-fall effect to the stomach‒ exhilarating once gotten used to. As for the head bobbing, it brings to mind dashboard figurines.

I've never seen anyone handle a car the way he does. In fact, it hadn't occurred to me a car could indeed be handled that way. I've seen people dance behind the wheel or swerve down the street, but Kevin… dances with the car. Every pump of the brake, every burst of acceleration, every jerk of the wheel, every shift our bodies made as a result; all came in perfect time with the music– no matter what type. Even when other drivers made false moves and forced him to stop short or swerve aside, this too was executed in a rhythmic fashion.

He seemed to enjoy switching lanes, moving through slower traffic and sliding in tight spaces. In no way is recklessness a part of it. Once, a swerving maneuver was aborted due to a sudden shift in traffic. I should've been at least jolted, but I could only nod my head and smile at the ingenious manner in which he'd handled the change; keeping his cool and still flowing to the music. I think it's cute– especially the way he tilts and bobs his head to the car's motion. He calls it "street surfing." No doubt, it's a style of driving no one practices, but one he's mastered. One which I've secretly come to like.

In short, Kevin has become a big part of my life, treating me unlike any before him. There are things about him that are… just different. He really pays attention to me, to everything I say as well as most of what I don't. With that heightened level of perception, where seemingly nothing escapes, he latches on to my slightest change of mood, asking whether I want to talk about it, if he sensed it to be troubling. Sometimes he even knows if I have to pee. Eerie, but I like it. It shows how into me he really is.

He surprises and showers me with gifts for no reason

than to see me smile, having said to me, once, the sadness I often conceal bleeds through, that I'm far more beautiful and sexually attractive when happy. He said this in my front room. We had recently returned from dinner at Dolphin Reef, and he'd just given me a diamond and emerald necklace with matching earrings. His statement of beautiful and sexually attractive said he was ready to accept what I'd been so eager to give.

I fell back on the couch, pulling him down on top of me to where we grinded and kissed passionately, his erection growing against me. The thought of him sliding in excited me, though not the usual anticipatory excitement I get in bringing Death to yet another. I underwent a woman's true longing for sex with a man she deeply wants, a response to what comes off as a silent promise of gratification. I waited to feel the slow removal of my clothes, but he held back.

"What we have here," he said. "Is the beginning of a nice friendship. Sex is easy to come by. What's hard is a woman I actually enjoy having around. I'm not asking you to fuck. Just continue to be who you are. I like you and don't want that to change."

Aroused only to be left unsated is a sensation I'm not the least bit fond of. I asked if fucking me was cause to like me less. He said sex, more times than not, led to complications. He kissed me again, and I thought sure he'd take me. He didn't. He up and left. I grew angry with him for leaving me in such a state. I don't understand what keeps him from fucking when it's obvious he wants to.

He has this lustful hunger in his eyes when he looks at me. And the way he kisses me is so breath-taking, done so passionately that I sometimes feel he's only seconds away from tearing my clothes off, but he stops short, leaving me breathless and desperately horny. He proclaims himself an observationist, never missing much. I agree with him in this, and sometimes wonder if that's what keeps him from going through with it; whether he somehow knows what I carry. Then I ask myself how, when I've spoken with no one about it, leaving no way for my secret to have gotten out. I have to rationalize that though he's being held back by something, it's not by conscious knowledge of the threat.

Aside from the way he constantly teases me with false promises of fulfillment, he's nice to be around. I never thought a person's presence could have such a dramatic effect on one's emotional state, but with Kevin I'm not as depressed as I am most of the time. The thought of poisoning others comes nowhere close to mind. And the thought of poisoning him is devastating. Though my goal had been to get him with Death, I can't even stomach the thought of doing this now.

I have a conscious when it comes to him. I feel as if I shouldn't bring Death to him; he doesn't deserve it. I felt something of this in the beginning, the day we first met. It grows continuously.

DEAR DIARY,

It's been about a week and a half since I've heard from Kevin, two weeks since I've seen him. The communication lapse between us resulted from a misstep on my behalf. Two weeks ago, Kevin's daily calls and frequent visits came to an abrupt halt. Four days went by– I heard nothing from him. I thought first of his occupation, that something may have happened to him. It even crossed my mind he may have gotten himself arrested. I got no calls from jail. My thoughts were of something worse, working the possibility of him having gotten himself killed or seriously injured and hospitalized, unable to communicate.

I called the county jail and every hospital in Savannah in search of him. I found myself paying closer attention to the news and reading the paper. Nothing there, my thoughts went elsewhere to thinking he may have found someone else to occupy his time, neglecting me in the process. I blew up in a fit of rage, emotions ranging from anger to concern, jealousy, betrayal; each having its share of dominion. "Pussy's no factor." he'd always said, and I had always believed him.

That in mind with all the attention he pays to me, I wondered what sort of woman could make him simply forget my existence. I concluded none— at least not so that he wouldn't call. Thus, my anger and jealousy fled in the face of concern, which later gave way to feelings of betrayal. For half a week, I was an emotional wreck. My days at work were a mess. I could hardly focus and recount what customers ordered.

Kevin must've decided he wanted nothing more to do with me, I began to think. I knew him to be a gentleman and just couldn't see him dropping someone like that, and so the cycle continued. By day four, I began feeling the weight of losing my life raft, for that's what Kevin has come to be. Depressive anger took the governing stand. Once again, I wanted to strike out. I poked a safety pin through several condoms in preparation of a night's charade of Death spreading. I wanted people to pay for how I felt, for them to someday feel my pain, isolation, and helplessness; the sense of pending doom while able to do nothing but suffer from it all.

I was nearly out the door when he rang my cell phone. He had time only to say he'd been out of town before I fired off a line of accusations, demanding to know who he'd been with. He let me finish. Then he said, ever so calmly, "Shawty why you trying me like that? Last time I checked we were only friends, which gives you no right to demand any explanation from me. I'm my own man. I answer to no one. Shawty we're not even fucking. Even if you were my wife, I wouldn't stand for what you just pulled. For the record, I've been out of town on business, alone. I missed your company. This call was to let you know I'd be there shortly, but that won't happen. I'll talk with you later." His call spared a lot of people that night, for I was too distraught to carry out the task.

That was a week and a half ago. There since, I've been waiting to hear from him. My sense of isolation presses in strong, and I have only myself to blame for his withdrawal. The second the call ended, I regretted my mistake and knew I'd never make it again if given the opportunity. In this, I came face to face with how deep my attraction is to him. I've been aware of it for a while, but never did I imagine hurting so at his refusal to see me.

This is new to me. Before my diagnosis—knowing myself to be honest, faithful, and trustworthy—I wouldn't have been the least concerned with a man's withdrawal; the loss would be more his than mine. Times have changed, though. I'm no longer such a marvelous gift; the goods are tainted. And with his counteractive affect to my depression, the loss is all mine; a definite blessing for him, however. I'm impatient for his anger to pass, for him to reestablish contact. I need him desperately. From the beginning, Kevin had insisted we remain friends, refusing sexual intimacy while reminding me to keep my emotions in check. In contrast, he treats me much like a beloved wife, with tenderness, gifts, time shared. In public, he holds me close, an image portraying us as lovers, caring neither for who saw nor for their thoughts. Alone, I'm in his arms receiving intimate caresses and kisses.

For all his understanding and perception, did he not

know that women are highly emotional creatures; I was sure to fall for him and cling possessively if threatened with separation? Actions speak louder than words, and mine were encouraged by his. It would be nice to have him realize he's partially responsible for what has him so upset. Yes, he seriously needs to come to his senses. I've been without him for two weeks, which is more than I can stand. I'll end this here; frustrated, alone, dying slowly.

DEAR DIARY,

Coming in from work, I opened my door to find Kevin in my front room waiting for me. I was stuck for a second, feeling everything from surprise to anger at the invasion. "Sorry for intruding," he said, staring me down. Like a baby girl missing her father, I wanted to fling myself into his arms. I fought the impulse and kept my cool, locking the door behind me, returning his stare.

He took my shoulders and kissed me. A light kiss it was, heavy with tender passion. He told me to have a shower, that we'd talk thereafter, and he gave no hint as to the subject. This is why I spent close to fifteen minutes in the shower with what possible matters. I was apprehensive near the end, fearing he may have stumbled across my diary, therefore, my secret. Impatient to know, I hurriedly dried myself, wrapped up in the towel, and fled to my room—to find Kevin in my bed, under the covers. His clothes were on the floor beside the bed. Needless to say, my diary remained undiscovered.

"Come here," he said, throwing back the covers and revealing his marvelous body. "Let's talk."

I slid in beside him, my pulse quickening with what's to come. I thought of all the times he'd kissed and caressed me to arousal. My mind held firm the vision of his naked body, visualizing him pushing inside of me. I grew excited laying there knowing it would soon come to pass. Always, his touch is so promising, so lust inducing. I've never wanted sex from anyone as bad as I wanted it from him. My pussy twitched in ways it never had before; a spasm just past the labia.

I found his hand and placed it to my stomach. He made slow, ever-widening motions over my abdomen. I ached for him to hurry, to touch me everywhere−I burned for it! He went for my breasts, stroking one then the other, missing no part of either. Adequate attention was paid to my nipples, which made me know he'd fuck me right, that I would truly enjoy it.

Propped up beside me, he leaned in to tongue my breast, simultaneously running a hand down my stomach. Having waited for months, my legs parted in welcome. His fingers slid between my lips, delving in deep. With two fingers he dragged moisture to my clit, rolling it gently between forefinger and thumb. Currents of bliss spiraled about. I moaned and sighed deep... Then he fell between my thighs and shattered the spell of passion.

The reluctance I felt at getting him with Death poured ten-fold; I didn't want to. The thought, on the rare occasion it did surface, was bothersome. Here, today, the prospect had me near to panic. I went still beneath him. He paused immediately, frowning down at me.

"Shawty," he said. "You've been trying to sex me for months, and here you freeze up like a scared virgin. You're no virgin, but I sense fear. Tell me what's wrong?"

I couldn't answer at first, so sudden had he popped the question. I told him it was only the simple matter of using protection. His hand came from under the pillow beneath my head bearing an empty Durex condom wrapper.

"One step ahead of you," he said, and I reached between us and felt him

He kissed me long, hard and deep before rolling onto his back, flipping me to where mine lay against his chest, my knees drawn up and feet to either side of him. He palmed my breasts and pinched my nipples, caressing my thighs and stomach. With one hand and a little arch from me, he guided himself inside, drawing from me a sigh of gratification. We were in a position which required my help considerably– one which should've left me in control, but he, instead, regulated the pace with sure hands on my hips.

My wide-spread legs gave him easy access to my clit, which he rubbed and pressed, enhancing the penetration. None before has given me such attention. Never have I had pleasure spring from so many places at once. I moaned in ways that sounded strange to my own ears. This multi-play of stimulation brought climax close quick. I fought against his controlling hands to move faster. He wouldn't have it. I continued to fight, trying in vain to come down on him harder, faster still. Countering my effort required both hands on my hips, leaving only his dick as sole provider of pleasure. I felt the loss, but climax was close–really close. I just knew I'd come regardless, if only I could break the tantalizingly steady pace he held me to. I put forth an even greater struggle, telling him how close I was to coming, begging him to oblige me.

Talk of this nature drives men wild. Most would eagerly comply. In this, Kevin proved different, ignoring my plea, maintaining restraint. His face to one side of mine, he whispered my name and told me faster is not always better, that if I followed his lead what I seek will hit harder than I ever thought possible. Of course I was hearing none of that. The beginning tremors of climax were nearly upon me. A few fast strokes and it'll surely hit hard. His lead could only be the opposite. I fought on. He nibbled my ear then asked that I trust him on this. He promised I wouldn't regret my decision in doing so. I couldn't see it. Couldn't imagine an orgasm being more powerful than what hovered before me. It hinted at nothing short of explosive. I wanted it.

Then it dawned on me that I hadn't reached my current state alone. Kevin had been the leading hand, the pilot transporting me. And I, destination in sight, wanted to wrest away control. His precision with most things came to mind and I knew he'd be on point here as well. The thought carried weight and still I had trouble convincing my body. Logic prevailed when he questioned, "How pleasant do you think it's gonna be with you opposing me?"

I settled to follow his lead. His hands, free from the task of keeping me in check, resumed their wondering caress, stroking my breast, massaging my clit, once again bringing to me that tri-mode level of stimulation. As he suggested, my movements were slow, rising almost all the way off before sliding ever so slowly down the length of him. His mouth warm at my ear and neck, his hands an ever-constant trail of fire igniting everything everywhere, all contributed to my unconscious attempt to go faster, whereas he'd coax me slower. Climax called from the horizon, and I wanted so badly to rush out and meet it.

I understood why men lost control and savagely pursued the hell out of climax. The faintest hint spawned a chase to the end. There was no help for it. I can only imagine the male begging the woman to wait for him just as climax shows her a piece of its face. She wouldn't wait.

Yes, if things were in reverse with him dependent upon her control, he'd find himself disappointed more times than not. Some women, like me, are potentially quick comers; two or three to his one. Then there're those who, after having one, care nothing for a second or third. Finding the first satisfactory, she wants only for him to be finished.

We, as women, have been spared the label of "selfish" and "inconsiderate" because we're the ones with the pussy enabling us to simply "lay there" or pretend once we've had our share. I haven't given it much thought before now, but had I ever been asked to wait, it would've been a futile request. Only Kevin's physical intervention kept me from plunging head long into oblivion.

Several times I was of a mind to savagely pursue its end. He played along my clitoris hood while running his fingers rapidly over the head. The combination made for an excruciating increase in pleasure, the effect metaphorically akin to 5.1 surround sound–translated to pleasure. That is, in the way external contact complemented that from within, encircling the region with currents of bliss, spiraling out to blissfully engulf every nerve ending. I screamed.

Kevin, with measured strokes to my clit, encouraged me to stay up top and keep it slow. With climax rushing in from the horizon, closer now than ever, I had serious trouble complying with his command. I wanted to ride that dick hard and fast, a speed to match that of his dancing fingers.

"Nice and slow," he instructed. "Now come down, that's it, all the way down. All the way."

I ground my ass hard into his pelvis, arching my back and taking him as deep as the position allowed. He held me there, unwilling to let me rise. His hold was verbal, yet I obeyed when every fiber of my being screamed to spring along that hot rod. I kept hard pressed to him, paying close attention to the finger working my clit. Several times I made efforts to rise. He countered with instructions not to.

"Kevin, please!" I moaned at one point. "It's right there—I can feel it! Let me have it, please! I can't do this your way!" He responded in telling me not to cheat myself, that in just a little while I'll have it like never before. I felt its closeness and wanted it that very instant. I wanted it my way. I also knew he would physically oppose me if I did not obey. To fight through climax would ruin the experience. But what was I to do? This was torture this was torture.

He gave me rein to rise, with instructions to work the head. I complied. And like before; the angle, complemented by dancing fingers, brought on the aforementioned surround effect with shocking intensity.

I took it upon myself to take him deep, keeping it slow as I knew he'd instruct. Somewhere through the second descent I felt its beginning. By the fourth, climax was fully upon me, every bit of what he'd promised; one like never before, hitting harder than I ever thought possible.

Screaming, I came down hard on him once, twice—

"You'll chase it away like that," Kevin intervened, a hand to my waist regulating my pace, the other having fell to a lighter, slower caress to my clit. I screamed for what seemed like forever as climax peeked, paused, and held for half eternity.

I've never had an orgasm stay so long. One normally last the length of a nice scream. Here, with this, I nearly choked twice in filling my lungs again and again, and still it remained. I've experienced the string orgasm before; one riding the back of another. This was no string, but one long soul-shaking orgasm, with infinite hang time. Kevin's grip tightened on my hip as climax came to him as well, fading away long before mine.

With its passing, I relaxed against him, totally spent, unable to move. He gave my breast an affectionate squeeze before circling his arms around me. For close to three minutes, we laid there in silence, my back to his chest, him half-hard inside me as I savored one of the greatest orgasms ever!

"Will you be my girl?" he asked, breaking the silence. "In every sense of the word. Faithfully?"

The question sped my slowing pulse. There was no mistaking the compatibility between us. We've sampled almost all of each other. Sex was one of the few things left unexplored. Having had it, his question, here, was whether it was enough. Be his girl? God knows I wanted nothing more. I felt as if the man of my dreams had just asked me to marry him. I wanted to jump up and down screaming yes, but I kept my cool while putting his own question back to him. I had to know if I were enough for him, that he'd honestly be faithful to me.

"I'm asking nothing more than I'm willing to give," he countered, kissing my neck. I said yes, while trying to reengage him. He wasn't for it. Expressing a desire to cook me dinner, he left the room whistling a merry tune. I nearly burst into laughter once I recognized the melody to be that from the Enzyte (male enhancement) commercial. I blushed furiously; glad he couldn't see my reaction. He's just so fucking wonderful!

DEAR DIARY,

For a week after the first time Kevin and I had sex, I feared his return to have been for nothing other than just that; and he'd leave once thoroughly paid. Being his girl is too good to be true; men simply aren't that compatible. At any moment I expect him to up and vanish—having got what he'd come for.

He remains consistent in the way he treats me. I feel… precious. When I consider how normal he makes life for me, the companionship and intimacy he provides, the thought of him leaving scares the hell out of me. I don't want to be alone. What's more is I have no way of showing my appreciation. Save loyalty and sex— both of which he has unconditionally— I have nothing to offer.

Speaking of sex, Kevin is by far the best I've ever slept with. I've always enjoyed being on top, but Kevin has made it a more enjoyable experience. He lets me ride until I'm close to coming, then I'll lean forward, and he'll do the rest; rising off the bed to thrust himself in me with hard, rapid strokes. The vibrations are similar to what's delivered when hit from behind. Only the penetrating angle is different.

He's yet to eat my pussy, but I'm sure he's good there also. The thought gets me horny. Kevin is sharp, and I'm quite sure he knows I want my pussy ate. He either wants me to straight out ask for it, or he has something in mind. I haven't given him head either, for that matter. He has only to ask, and I'll suck him dry. There's nothing I won't do for him.

As for my Circle of Death… I'm no longer ruining people's lives in that fashion. It should never be mistaken that I bear any regret for what I've done. Aside from the fact that I don't cheat, I'm not feeling that sort of thing right now. At the same time, I need not say there are ways other than sex when it comes to getting one with Death. I know several. I'm just not currently inclined. Other than that occasional nightmare where I'm chased by that dark shadow, everything is fine. Life for me is simple. I'm happy.

DEAR DIARY,

Today was nearly tragic. I came in from work to have Kevin, hiding behind the door, pounce on me, toss me around, and tear at my clothes. I screamed and pretended to be frightened by his intent. We've played this game before. It's one much to my liking.

Once naked, I'd scream "No, help, stop, don't!" He would curse at me and say how the pussy was his; that he'd soon have it and there was nothing I could do to stop him. The closer he came to subduing me, the more frantic I'd pretend to be, struggling wildly. This is a real turn-on for me. Though he's truly the stronger, entry is never forced. He allows me to dictate the moment of penetration. There's no telling what position we'd end up in. At times, he'll pin my knees to my chest and take me that way. Other times, I'll find myself on all four, neck crammed against the headboard, with my ass in the air. At some point I'd reduce the level of resistance, and then only would he fight his way in. He's both fair and patient in this game, allowing me to suddenly break free to begin the fight anew. He would again subdue me in yet another position. Things get knocked over throughout, but we try and minimize what's broken.

Today, after a fierce struggle, Kevin managed to secure a position between my thighs. I had my hands down between us, protecting my treasure, blocking his entrance. Snarling, he pawed at my protection. I squirmed and bucked half-heartedly. Ready to have it, I let him tear my hands away. Hot flesh grazed my fingers. In that instant I knew he wore no condom. Before I knew what happened, with a sudden burst of strength, I screamed and kicked out from beneath him.

The scream held true terror, which gave him pause to consider. He asked if he'd somehow hurt me, unaware. His frown deepened with my answer of no. I silently cursed my dramatic response, all the while praying he wouldn't sense anything amiss. I had no excuse for my behavior. All I could think to do is express my discomfort at the idea of sex unprotected. It stunned me to hear him speak of his want to feel me raw, his promise not to get me pregnant. I handed him a condom and told him that pulling out is not assurance enough for me. For now, we should do it the right way.

He was quick to comply, respecting my decision. Instead of the ruff act we were seconds away from, he sexed me slow, kissing me with tender passion. It felt as if he were trying to convey his love through actions of body. I clung tight, consumed by dreadful thoughts of what had barely been avoided. A stroke of luck is all that brought my fingers in contact with his flesh, preventing tragedy. I cried silently, and to his question of why, I said only that I loved him.

Always before, if he were to pounce, he'd have on a condom so as not to break stride, come time for penetration. Today he'd pounced without, expressing a desire to feel me raw when caught. I, too, would like to have it raw, even for him to come inside me, but the price is not worth it. The thought of poisoning Kevin tears at my heart in ways I can't explain. Had it been anyone else, they would've gotten their wish. A stroke of luck is all that saved him.

DEAR DIARY,

I couldn't imagine anything worse than being told you're HIV positive and knowing your ex as the one responsible. Two days ago, when Kevin left town on business to Florida, I discovered there is worse.

Kevin knows I worry when he's away. Thus, he's come to calling periodically to assure me of his well-being. His number showed on the caller ID, bringing a smile to my face, excited just in seeing his name. Almost laughing, I answered his call− and got the second shock of my life. From his end of the line came the unmistakable sounds of passion, a woman wailing in ecstasy, one being thoroughly worked over.

In that instant two things were clear: Kevin was fucking, and he had mistakenly speed dialed my number in the process, providing me with more than I wanted to hear. My smile died. Anger, betrayal, disbelief, jealousy and hurt fell in on an unprecedented scale. God himself is wrong for allowing us to hurt to such a degree. For those first few minutes, Death would've been a welcome reprieve. Nothing should ever hurt that bad– not emotionally.

Often, he's told me that pussy is no factor; that he wouldn't cheat, that I'd be enough. I believed him and would've continued to do so, had I not heard with my own ears the heart stopping truth. Numb to the bone, I listened until it became too much to bear. I ended the call in tears, finding it extremely difficult to breathe. I cried for nearly two hours before gathering the shattered pieces of my heart and hardening myself to the pain– a pain which now falls in the dominant shadow of vengeful anger.

"To have me is to have Death." I once said this for all who sexed me. All with the exception of Kevin. Hurting him that way has never set well with me from the start. On rare occasions when the thought surfaced, I panicked, felt fear, felt choked by the concept. Over time, the thought became truly petrifying. When finally he took me to bed, I did my best in providing the utmost gratification while secretly maximizing protection; ensuring condoms were fresh and never "casually forgotten."

I now ache to get him with Death. The thought, just as with others before, fills me with anticipatory excitement. He said there would be no other! And for me to find out like this... Even now I cry silently, fresh tears falling down my face to stain this very page. I would've taken this a lot better had I known there'd be others; the discovery would've triggered nothing more than a brief spark of jealousy, something gotten over quickly enough.

But, in the ways of men, he professed loyalty while exercising infidelity. He gave me nothing to cushion the blow. In times like this, I understand why women do nasty shit to men. It makes me hate that we're so careful when it comes to cheating, with our what-he-don't-know-won't-hurt outlook. I think women should be a bit more careless with it, so that men may stumble upon the truth more often. They deserve it.

I'm of a mind to get him with Death the moment he returns, but I've thought to make a little game of it. I won't offer damaged condoms, nor will I ever attempt to cause one to break during sex. Never again, though, will I remind him to wear one. Never again will I say no to his silent request to enter me raw. He aches to fuck me raw. In this, he'll bring Death to himself. It's not anticipatory excitement that the thought brings, but something more like grim satisfaction.

DEAR DIARY,

Kevin returned from Florida approximately four days ago and presented me with a platinum and diamond DKNY designer watch. I was extremely excited at his appearance, and it had nothing to do with his expensive gift. I truly missed him. I had no idea as to what extent until he showed up. Even so, I was still angry. The urge to get him with Death remained. I was puzzled about it, however. Some part of me wanted to go through with it, while the other opposed the notion. I felt that familiar sense of dread in contemplating the act.

I couldn't believe it. I'd never cringed at the thought of getting anyone with Death. In fact, there was always an anticipatory sense of excitement which made me want to do it, and the act was never less than ecstatic. Kevin is the exception in this. From the beginning, the thought of getting him with Death didn't sit well with me. The longer I associated myself with him, the more opposed to the idea I'd become until the very thought of harming him drove me to panic. He'd become my world. My source of life. I'd come to love him fiercely.

Then he goes out and cheats. To me that is the ultimate betrayal. It is how Death was brought to me in the first beginning. I expected better from Kevin. He swore to me that he would touch no other, that he would be faithful. The fact he'd lied and has done otherwise should have nullified any feelings I harbored against getting him with Death. With his betrayal, I should ache to get him with Death.

Why then, after he'd presented his gift and I was held within his embrace, did I stiffen at his expressed desire to possess me? Why was I nearly torn to pieces at the mere mentioning of sex? As is the case with Kevin and his master perception, he noticed the changed immediately. He paused in his caressing of me and frowned as he looked me over.

"You're never less than eager to accommodate my advance," he said to me. "Are you on your period?"

"No," I said.

His frown deepened. "Then what's bothering you, princess. You seem so… unyielding… reluctant."

I was far from unyielding or reluctant. The truth of the matter is I was overwhelmingly excited at the prospect. Excited in the way a woman is when the man she loves seeks pleasure with her and she, too, is in the mood. After overhearing his infidelity, I had been certain I'd never again know such excitement. The reluctance he sensed was my unwillingness to get him with Death. This came as a surprise to me. I said I wouldn't give him damaged condoms nor make any attempt to break one during sex. I also said I'd never again stop him from sexing me raw, something he attempts and pleads for with increasing frequency. He would step into the arms of Death on his own accord. Why, then, did I freeze and panic? The desire to let him slip, remains– as does my reluctance to go through with it.

I stood torn in his arms with no acceptable answer. I wanted him to make love to me, and yet feared he would try it raw. At the same time, I feared I'd do nothing to stop him. After all, he'd betrayed me, and I was still angry. My love for him, I realized, was far greater than I'd allowed myself to believe. The fact I had qualms about getting him with Death while knowing his betrayal, was credence to the matter.

Seconds passed before I told him I was merely distracted by personal problems I wish not to discuss. I relaxed and responded to him with my usual passion. It wasn't until we were naked, and he had on a condom, did I truly become wild and indulgent with him. It came to me, then, how tense I'd been, that I'd been silently praying for the use of protection. For three days he stayed over, and every encounter filled me with tension, but in every session he wore a condom. Funny, but that in itself was gratifying. The stress was nearly too much, and I constantly wondered at my distraught in getting him with Death when it's what he's earned.

I was at war with myself, torn between vengeance and my desire never to hurt him. Though I tried to play it cool, Kevin knew something was amiss and was persistent in his attempt at coaxing me to address the matter. I held firm in my refusal. What could I say? I'm having trouble with the idea of giving him Death?

"I have some business that needs tending," Kevin said to me early this morning after fixing me breakfast. "I'll be away for two days, three at the most. By then you should have come to terms with what's bothering you. I can't stand to see you this way." He kissed me and was gone.

My resolve strengthens. By his return, I will have dealt with what plagues me. I'm more determined now than ever to let him reap the consequence of his action. He has betrayed me and must pay. It's just that simple. No more qualms about it. At his return, no longer will I be torn when he takes me to bed. Whether he uses a condom or not will be of no further concern to me. It was him who cheated, not I. Besides, I've told him repeatedly to wear protection with me. It's not my responsibility to continuously remind him. It's not my fault if he chooses not to protect himself.

DEAR DIARY,

Life as I've come to know it has come to an end. Absent for two days, Kevin returned and brightened my world in dedicating his time to me. The excitement he brings with only his presence is something I can never get used to, can never get enough of. No presence has ever affected me this way, and I never want to be without it.

We visited Oakland Island's Wildlife Conservation, strolling a wood plank trail through areas of woods, marsh, and grassland; observing various animals in their simulated habitat. We concluded the day with a late dinner at Johnny Harris.

Back at my place, we showered together, washing each other's back. We rinsed, and he gripped my ass. The contact was more sexual than casual, and my senses were super alert. At his return, I mentioned before, no longer would I be torn at the prospect of getting him with Death; I'd let him sex me raw if he chose. The suds ran down my body, chased away by the flowing water from the head.

Kevin's finger slid between my cheeks and he fingered me from behind. For long seconds he was at it, his fingers going deeper inside me. I stood there in silence, neither encouraging nor discouraging his efforts.

His probing became insistent with him inserting a second finger. I expected, at any moment, for him to bend me over and take me from behind right where we stood. I didn't panic, nor did I experience apprehension at the thought. I merely waited for him to act. The decision would be his. He would have only himself to blame.

Fortunately– for him, of course– he refrained from taking me. We toweled each other dry and fell naked in bed together. There was no sex between us, only gentle touching and cuddling that went on for some time before he lay still and was asleep. I followed shortly after.

Sometime during the night, I was awakened by Kevin's kissing and breathing on the back of my neck. His breath was hot, pleasantly stirring me to consciousness and longing. His dick was hard, pressing against my ass. Spooned behind me, his knees were tucked behind mine. A hand came around to cup my breast and pulled me closer as he kissed my neck and shoulder.

His dick slid past my cheeks and between my thighs seeking entry –and suddenly I was wide awake. I screamed and rolled away, tearing ferociously out of his embrace as if his dick had been a hot branding rod against my flesh. I was on the floor and he was peering down over the side of the bed before I realized what I'd done.

"What is wrong with you?" he asked.

I was terrified and angry at him for what he'd come so close to doing. I could have let him push right in and reap his reward of Death. Instinct had spurred me otherwise. I sat there perplexed, staring up at him and wondering at my unbidden reaction. The nigga had cheated and had yet to confess or apologize for it. For that he should be punished. So why couldn't I carry out the act— or simply lay there and let him do it to himself? With that, I was forced to face the facts; I was still happy and in love with him. I wanted to forgive and forget his error.

I knew then I could never get him with Death. It wasn't my true desire to do so. I honestly don't think that I can successfully live with giving him Death. What little sanity I have left would be destroyed. At all costs he must be protected. I knew then what I must do. He would leave me for certain, and considering his effect on me and every part of my life, how was I to live with that? In this my love had become my weakness, my undoing.

From the floor I glared up at him, angry for what must be. Angry that he wouldn't comply with my wish for protected sex at all times. I, too, craved raw sex with him and knew the act would be more explosive than what it was already. I couldn't fault him for trying when he had no idea it would bring about his demise. The blame could only be placed at my feet.

Kevin extended a hand and hauled me onto the bed beside him. Barring the moment I was diagnosed, the next few with Kevin were the worse ever in life. He circled his arms about my shoulders and I gently removed them from around me. I didn't want to feel his rejection once he heard what I had to say.

I took a deep breath. "Kevin," I said. "How many times

have you tried to fuck me raw?"

He shrugged. "I've lost count."

"And how many times have I stopped you?"

"Every single time," he replied. "You seem to be a bit stingy with it raw."

"And why do you think that is?"

"You're terrified of getting pregnant." He expressed moderate humor at the statement.

"Kevin, baby, I love you, and would like nothing more than for you to fuck me raw, for you to get me pregnant, for me to have your baby."

"But?" he prodded.

"It's…hazardous." I supplied.

He stared at me in silence, putting the pieces together. "What is it exactly?" he asked finally. "Herpes?"

I braced myself and told him it was HIV, and as I said the words I felt him slide away from me.

He was furious. "You mean you've been fucking me all this time and you have AIDS?"

I told him it wasn't AIDS, but HIV.

"What's the fucking difference?" he shouted. "One becomes the other and then you die!"

He asked what I had been thinking in fucking him for so long and saying nothing. He jumped to his feet and went over to a drawer, snatching out clothes with which to dress, again with the question why didn't I tell him. I told him I loved him more than I ever loved anyone or anything in life. That I've known unprecedented happiness since meeting him. That I've ascended from a world of darkness in being with him.

"The sadness you once used to catch in my unguarded

moments," I pointed out, "derives from me knowing and having to deal with what fate has dealt me. It's a fate none can change. But you–you counter the effects of my reality." In light of that, I asked how could he expect me to give that up. How could he expect me to tell him when the result would be him leaving, my world returned to what it had been before, a darkened void of emotional chaos.

"So why now?" he asked.

"I have no choice," I told him. "At every turn you're trying to fuck raw. You mean the world to me. I could never do anything to hurt you, but you won't comply; what other choice is there?"

Completely dressed, he came to stand before me. He took both my hands in his and pulled me to my feet, looking over my nakedness. He turned me about, completing his survey. He locked gazes with me, and after a while, told me I was beautiful, perfect. Mentally and physically.

"I told myself that there was nothing that could ever make me let you go," he said. "But I never considered this. The scary thing is no one can tell by looking at you. He would never guess."

He kissed me then, long and passionate. I returned the kiss, knowing it would be the last from him, that it was goodbye. He released me, and I clung to him a moment longer, reluctant to let go. I cried silently, tears running down my face.

"I'm sorry," he told me. "I'm not trying to be cruel–I would never do that to you–but I can't do this. It's way too much for me."

"I know," I told him. "I understand, and the fucked-up

thing is I can't even beg you to stay."

He left then and has been gone now for about an hour. I've been crying since. I'm no fool. This isn't me misbehaving and pissing him off, or something to briefly irritate a relationship. The barrier is permanent, an irreparable rift between two people. An attitude I can change or adjust. My diagnosis, however, will never change– except from HIV to that of AIDS. With that, I feel I'll never see him again.

DEAR DIARY,

I went to Citi Trends, today, shopping for a couple of new outfits. It isn't as if I need any, or that I have any special occasion on which to wear them. It's that I've done nothing but come home from work and mope around my apartment from the moment Kevin walked out on me close to a month ago. Kenya has made attempts to lift my spirit, but nothing seems to work. Weed helps but it's only a mild suppressant. More times than not it enhances vivid memories of times with Kevin, down to the very emotions present at that moment. It's an experience I can very much do without.

Shopping, however, is something else I like, and today I decided to make it a step towards rehabilitation. With that, I was bent over browsing through a rack of jeans when the light was partially blocked as someone approached and stood next to me.

"Well," said the newcomer. "If it isn't the Prowling Jungle Cat." Though I couldn't remember his name, I knew who I'd see even before I straightened to acknowledge him. He was the guy from Club Sensation who'd followed me around for half the night, some months back, trying to fuck. I'd been on my period that night and for that reason only he'd been spared. I had to flat out tell the nigga I was bleeding in order for him to cease with his pursuit. I was curious at his persistence, however, and when asked he said I seem something exotic and forbidden− "a prowling jungle cat," were his exact words.

The description was something flattering. I liked it. I offered him good advice that night, suggesting he pursued no women he perceived as exotic, beautiful, or alluring if there was anything forbidden or dangerous associated with her. I told him I was especially included within that category. That being the case, I figured he'd offer no more than casual conversation as I turned to greet him today in Citi Trends.

"You're looking as good as ever," he said. "Though a bit sad. I can think of several things to brighten up your day. For starters, I'll buy you that dress I saw you sweatin."

I was startled by the guy's accurate assessment, as I had been the night we met in the club. I smiled with genuine humor at his attempt to get at me. The guy was funny without trying to be, and likeable. Not in the romantic sense, but more like a partner or homeboy. Not that the idea of romance was excluded, however; the nigga was fine. I asked was it his habit or common practice for him to ignore sound advice.

"You mean that lil bit about dangerously exotic women and leaving them alone?" he asked.

I was surprised he remembered. "Exactly," I said.

"I took your advice," he insisted. "I thought about that shit for weeks.

"I can't tell," I countered, "with you pushing up on me looking for more than conversation. I told you I was included in that category."

"Are you one of those fatal attraction types?" he asked.

"I can be," I told him. "I can make you wish you never met me."

"Such behavior has to be triggered, doesn't it?" he asked. "I'm usually well behaved if she's worth it." He said he would play fair with me if I'd only give him the chance. He tagged along behind me chatting away as I made my way around the store and back to the area where hung the dress in question. I pulled it from the rack and turned meaningfully.

"You know how much, right?" I asked, and his eyes widened with pleasant surprise, having had no idea I'd accept, expecting to be put off as he'd been that night at the club.

"If everything is understood," his gaze, if not his words, was clear. "The price don't matter."

I've yet to get anyone with Death since being with Kevin, and being pursued by this guy—Dameon, he reminded me—I was warming to the idea. My life was gloomy and dull, and the buzzing sense of pleasure in getting someone with Death is one kind of excitement I could use in my life. He was indeed brightening my day and it had nothing at all to do with him purchasing the dress.

He walked me to my car, and I gave him my cell number, informing him he wasn't dealing with the average woman, that he should consider carefully before calling. It was my final warning. He admitted to having given careful consideration for months, having thought continuously of catching up to me and making it happen. I was flattered by his admission, but I also knew a momentary ache for the guy in that he would get more than he'd bargained for.

In another life we probably would have gotten along well with something of an extensive relationship. What with the circumstances now, he will call, and I will go to him and pass my sentence of Death under the cover of bliss. Thereafter, I could care less if I ever saw him again.

DEAR DIARY,

Dameon called around eight-thirty and gave me his address in Cloverdale, asking if I'd come over to have a drink and some Kush with him. At the mentoring of Kush, I knew he wanted me fucked up. We both understood it wasn't necessary, that by mutual assent I was obligated to answer his summon. With the weed and drink, I realized, he wanted his money's worth. Whereas a simple fuck would conclude our business, he wanted me throughout the night. The drink and Kush would tie me to his bed until morning. I was game, though, and was ranging his doorbell some thirty minutes later.

Dameon opened the door to embrace and kiss me as if I was his girl instead of someone he'd propositioned only hours before. He seemed reckless with sex, the type who leapt in head first. Though I was well kept in appearance and physically appealing, he had no way of telling whether I was a nasty slut or any way of knowing I carried Death. I could tell by the way he kissed me that he would throw all caution out the window and fuck me raw. I wouldn't have to concern myself with giving him damaged condoms or sabotaging any protection he sought to use. The idea was a bit disheartening in that I've come to enjoy the challenge of breaking down their barriers, of getting them with Death while they were under the misconception of being protected.

He was a thirsty, lustful son of a bitch, all over me on the porch to the point I thought he'd strip me naked and fuck me right there. "I thought for a second you wouldn't come," he said, backing off and ushering me into his house. He seemed obsessed with having me there and I wondered if he'd go all out and eat my pussy. God knew I wanted him to.

He poured me a mixed drink of Alize and Hennessey. The weed was rolled, and we smoked. Halfway through the blunt he received a phone call. There were previous callers but he'd simply looked at the screen and sent them to voice mail. With this call, however, he looked at the screen, then offered an apology.

"It's my ace," Dameon said. "He's been seeing some girl for months now. According to him she's the most precious thing that walks the planet. She can't be all that, though; she caused the separation. Been about a month now. He's sick and the girl−whoever the hell she is− has him fucked up. We grew up together and I've never seen him like this over any female. He's stressing hard and nothing takes his mind off her."

"Why don't you invite him over to join us," I suggested as he answered the phone. He arched his brows. I nodded and winked. Joint in hand I took to looking around his living room, leaving him to speak with his ace. I was browsing over the pictures on his mantle when one in particular caught my attention; an enlarged photo taken at Frozen, a popular club in downtown Savannah. In it were two handsome males expensively dressed and standing shoulder to shoulder. The first figure was Dameon. Smiling broadly, he held a bottle of Moet in his right hand while flossing for the camera his left wrist where he sported a pricey looking diamond watch. The second figure, also adorned with pricey jewelry, was all seriousness in his pose. He, too, held a Moet bottle, but there was no smiling and flaunting of jewelry.

I was totally mesmerized by the occupants of the picture. I couldn't take my eyes off it. In fact, I was still staring when Dameon slid in close behind me, caressing my thighs.

"Who is that?" I asked, indicating the person in the picture beside him.

"That's my ace," he said. "I just invited him over. He's on the way now. He straight?"

More than nice. I thought of Kevin and was utterly sick with panic. I wanted out of there fast. I slid out from his embrace and went to snatch up my purse from the sofa.

"You know," I said to Dameon. "I don't think it was a good idea for me to come here tonight. Maybe we can do this some other time." Of course I was lying. Though Kevin and I weren't together, I wouldn't betray him by having sex with Dameon. Once I was out of that door, Dameon would never see me again. I think he knew this as well, for suddenly he was between me and the door. He asked what my problem was. If it was that I didn't want to see his boy, I didn't have to. He would call and tell him not to come.

I tried to assure him that wasn't the problem; the timing wasn't right. At that, the look in his eyes reminded me of the guy in the explorer who'd forced me under gunpoint while on my period. Staring at Dameon, I knew I would again be subjected to similar treatment.

"I don't know what your problem is, Shawty," he said to me. "But you better get your head right." He grabbed me by the shoulder and pushed me down onto the couch, saying I was the kind of girl who knew the rules in coming to a man's house, and the games I was playing were unacceptable. "Besides, Shawty, you owe me and I'm not letting you walk out on me like that."

I opened my purse and told him I'd pay for the dress, the weed, and the drink. He snatched my purse, closed it and tossed it aside. He didn't want my money. He had no use for it. He said he'd wanted me for too long only to have me come in and walk right out, as was my attempt. He extracted a wad of bills from his pocket and peeled off several hundred dollars, informing me it was mine if only I'd let it happen.

It wasn't about money, I told him, and neither was I atempting to play games. The timing wasn't right. I stood and made as if to pass him and was caught with a backhand that sent me sprawling to the couch. I tasted blood in my mouth and once again was reminded of my experience in the explorer. I knew fear, as I know rage. The beating would be rough, no doubt, but I wouldn't have to endure it if only I'd submit. I refused submission, however, and unlike the guy with the explorer, Dameon had no gun with which to subdue me.

I leapt to my feet and charged with arms swinging. He sidestepped, ducked, and was somehow behind me with arms about my waist. I was lifted and slammed hard onto the floor. I was rolled and pinned as he worked to unfasten my jeans.

"Come on, Shawty," he said. "There's no win for you like this. Why don't you just lay there and let me handle my business."

I was so fucking mad at the nigga for trying me with all that. The funny thing is he had no idea how bad I wanted to let him have just what the fuck he was begging for, but submission was betrayal; Kevin would never understand—no matter the circumstances. There would forever be the question of whether some part of me truly wanted the experience, such was human nature.

For the way in which Dameon treated me, I wanted with every fiber of my being to engage the act, but in no way for sexual gratification. My loyalty to Kevin wouldn't allow me to submit. Not even to get him with Death. Not even to spare myself a beating I would much rather do without.

With that, I struck out at him with my fist. He retaliated by slapping me twice and throttling my throat. "Shawty," he said. "I should really fuck you up for playing with me, but I'm not gone do that." He squeezed harder at my throat and my eyes felt as if they were going to pop out of their sockets. "Your choice," he said.

Angry at his ultimatum, I struck out with my fist. He shook his head and frowned at my rebellion. The pressure at my throat persisted. It was frightening to have the life choked out of me, to watch everything fuzz and fade to black. I became angry at Kevin for having to experience the trauma. If he hadn't chickened out and ran off on me the way he had, the likes of what Dameon visited upon me would have never come to pass. The ordeal was unlike any I've known in life…

I regained consciousness with gentle slaps on my face. My last memory of being choked, I struck out at the figure above me. My wrists were seized, my name was called, and I was told to calm down, that everything was alright. Though confused, I ceased my struggles. It wasn't the words I obeyed, but the voice instead. My vision cleared and I was able to focus on the face staring down at me. An observation of the room revealed Dameon on the couch glaring as Kevin helped me to my feet.

It was obvious my love had arrived to thwart Dameon's attempt. And from the looks of the other's swollen jaw, Kevin had been forceful in the matter. My pants were down at my knees, and I pulled them up and fastened them quick. Kevin snatched up my purse and handed it to me. We left with his arm around my shoulders. I had the impression he'd escort me to my car then see me off. Instead, he took my keys, ushered me into the passenger seat and climbed in behind the wheel.

"So," Kevin broke the silence. "Why did you refuse him?"

"Why did you stop him?" I countered.

"From which do you mean? Rape? Or what he would have contracted as a result? I don't condone rape, and the idea of anyone knowingly giving a person HIV is heartless. It's inhumane. Yet there are those who do it. Considering the fact you were opposed to his advance, he would've gotten more than what he'd bargained for, what he would have deserved for that behavior. But you were buckin'; I understood you were all for it and then some."

Men aren't happy, to say the least, when their girl or the woman they have feelings for sleeps with a friend or family member. It's the ultimate betrayal. Pride is wounded and men are hurt. Although Kevin had walked out on me, he would have known these sentiments had I committed the act. I conveyed this to him along with the fact I'd seen him in a picture with Dameon.

Hearing that, he divided his attention between me and the road. "You truly know the game, don't you?" I didn't know what to say to that. However, I admitted to Kevin that had it not been for him, I wouldn't have taken that beating, and Dameon would have been up shit creek. He shot me an apprehensive look. "You're angry, aren't you? Not about tonight. I mean .... about your diagnosis?"

"Angry at the world," I admitted and was suddenly sobbing uncontrollably in both frustration and anger. He rubbed my neck and shoulder, offering words of comfort. I was too distraught to make out all he said, but I surely heard him mention something about psychiatric counseling to help deal with the matter, that he'd be with me every step of the way.

He parked in my driveway and the car was left running as he escorted me to my door, leaving me with the promise of his return before sunrise. That was over an hour ago and I've since had a shower and some time to think about his suggestion. I've never considered psychiatric treatment and I'm not so sure it will help. Not only that. I'm not so sure it's something I want. I've come to trust Kevin's judgment, so I'll go along. He loves me and wants what's best. He said my happiness becomes his. I feel the same.

Though my body aches from being slammed to the floor, my jaw bruised and swollen at being slapped around, the pain pales in comparison to the bliss I feel at having Kevin back. The experience was every bit worth the outcome. With my secret revealed, there's nothing to threaten our relationship. No longer will I know panic or have to worry about accidently getting him with Death. Fate has finally dealt me a hand worth playing. Maybe there is a shot at happiness in my future.

DEAR DIARY,

Weeks have come and gone since Kevin had come to Dameon's recue. I can see it as nothing other than that. For it had truly been Dameon's welfare in jeopardy that night. True to his word, Kevin had returned before sunrise that morning, and I was waiting in bed, anxious for his love making, but he didn't lay a finger on me. Not sexually, however. Instead, he climbed into bed beside me and expressed our need for open conversation. He promised not to hold anything against me as long as I remain totally honest with him. He wanted nothing hidden between us. No more surprises which could upset our relationship

I was extremely nervous, weary of what he may ask. He wanted to know how long have I been infected, how it happened, who was responsible, and where was he currently. At the last question I hesitated, but reasoned that Kevin is from the streets, in part, and he wouldn't snitch if I confided in him. I told him everything surrounding David and Jasmine's death.

He was astounded; having seen the news surrounding the incident, he had simply believed, as had the authorities, the girl had gone berserk in murdering the boyfriend and had taken her own life thereafter. The Headlines had dubbed it "An extreme case of kink" and "A crime of passion." He also wanted to know if I'd been intimate with anyone other than him, since our beginning.

I chose that moment to seek answers of my own, putting to question his fidelity. I brought to his attention the night on which I received that heart shattering call with the unmistakable act of sex in the background. He was utterly perplexed in the matter, and it irked me that he appeared genuine with it. I pointed out the exact date and time which the call had come. His expression towards me, then, is one I'd never gotten from him; incredulity, and it bothered me to see that.

He brightened all of a sudden and was all smiles and excitement. He jumped out of bed and disappeared into the bathroom, returning seconds later with his BlackBerry, that which he eagerly handed over, pointing near the edge—where there had once been a crack, the result of me getting out of his car and dropping the phone from my lap.

I remember well the day it happened. I thought the phone destroyed and was weary of his displeasure, apologizing even as I recovered the phone. He had assured me that it wasn't a problem, that he'd get another. It hadn't been destroyed in the fall but had suffered a crack on the right corner.

The BlackBerry in which he'd thrust into my hand was the same model, minus the crack. He'd purchased a new one while in Florida, he said; the old one having been misplaced or stolen. Same number, different phone. The call in question, he said, had to have come the night on which the phone was lost.

"For a second, there," Kevin said to me. "I thought you were losing your mind and tripping out real hard." He held me close in a manner of relief. He was glad to have put my mind at ease. He reminded me that he wouldn't cheat, that he'd be man enough to talk with me if his attention was to stray.

I attempted to engage him when the conversation was over, but he declined on the grounds the day had been long and so had the night. It was early morning and he needed rest. Fact is I can't remember Kevin being anything less than accommodating if not the first to engage. We slept and woke late in the afternoon. Here, again, he brushed aside my attempt, stressing business to be taken care of. He kissed me, dressed quick and was gone, leaving me to finger myself with only the memory for stimulation. The orgasm was weak and unfulfilling, there being no substitute for Kevin.

I spent the day in agitation, awaiting his return. I know Kevin's desire for me and knew, upon his return, he'd be more than eager to accommodate me, having taken care of business. Kenya came by, observing my healthier attitude as well as my agitation and was quick to question the latter. She laughed at my revelation but didn't miss the opportunity to try me in offering to assist where Kevin declined. I'm used to her advances and find them quite humorous at times, though her seriousness in the matter is never to be questioned. That being the case, I'm ever careful not to lead her on, consistent in my refusal to go there with her. This day, however, Kenya was persistent in her advance.

"Why not?" she asked. "If you're embarrassed about it, I'll keep it on the low. I won't put you out there. It will be our secret." I expressed how it wasn't that I'd be ashamed or embarrassed, only that I had no interest in women. I was tempted to tell her I had my own pussy to play in, my own breast to touch, and my own ass to feel, but I knew she'd counter with several facts I couldn't dispute. One being that I couldn't lick my own pussy.

We went to Keith's Crab House and brought garlic crabs and shrimp, retuning to my place to watch TV while smoking a blunt, that which was burning near to its end when Kevin returned. I nearly pushed Kenya out the front door in that she knew well my desire and teasingly took her time about leaving.

Alone with Kevin, in no way was I subtle with my intent. He wouldn't go for it, however. Even at my persistence he bucked. Under no circumstances would he let himself be seduced. Shamelessly, I followed him around the house; all over him as would a hungry predator on prey. His frustration was something I didn't care to acknowledge. He sat on the living room couch and I fell on top of him. I was naked down to panties and bra.

Astride him, kissing him, I felt his arousal and thought I'd succeeded in my seduction. Then, firm but gentle, he gripped my shoulders and held me back, holding my gaze. "Now is not a good time," he said before lifting me off him and sitting me aside as if my weight to him was no more than a child's. From beneath the couch, he pulled out the carrycase containing his laptop. I knew any further attempt would be unwanted harassment. It confirmed my suspicion, however. I left him alone and went to bed.

Torn, I curled up under the covers and tried not to cry. This attitude had never been directed at me, and regardless of what excuse he gave, the truth in the matter is with my diagnosis. Having knowledge of it, he was afraid to touch me. He stayed on the laptop for hours and didn't come to bed 'til late. I was so afraid of further rejection, by then, I didn't even try. He gathered me close, kissed me, and was soon fast asleep. It didn't go un-noticed that he wore boxer to bed when normally he'd sleep naked. I tossed and turned for most the night and he was gone when I awoke the next morning.

Unable to hold suppress further, I cried. It was too much for me. His actions said all that his words did not. His rejection was a constant reminder of my diagnosis. It countered the natural effect of his presence and filled me with misery instead. It was worse than being alone. I knew he loved me. For that reason alone he had returned. But having the one who loves you unwilling to bed you is something disheartening. It's perfectly understandable when one is busy or simply not in the mood. It's something else entirely when your lover is literally terrified of having sex with you. I've known some very disturbing emotions in the past, but none measured up to this.

The rejection went on for nearly two weeks until my depression became anger, and I forced a confrontation. He was on the couch in the living room tapping at the keys of his laptop when suddenly I snatched it away from him. He shot to his feet, surprised. I closed the laptop and tossed it on the chair behind me, positioning myself between him and the distractions.

"What the fuck is your problem," he said, attempting to go around me for the laptop.

I sidestepped to intercept and shoved him backward, equally angry. "What the fuck is *your* problem?" I countered. He knew what bothered me and didn't pretend otherwise. He sighed, sat down on the couch, and held open his arms to me. Neither one of us wanted to fight about it. I went to him, and for long moments he held me in silence. My respect for him grew in that he made no pretense about what hung between us, no attempt to argue and flip the script.

"Baby," he said to me. "I'm pretty good at figuring things out and working through complicated situations. I delve to the source in order to find a possible solution. The simple truth is I'm scared." He admitted to having gotten himself tested three times at three different clinics during the month of our separation. He said he loved me no less, but he was utterly terrified of contracting the virus. The idea of sex with me is like flirting with Death. I didn't know what to say, but I imagined the shoe being on the other foot and couldn't see myself willingly having sex with a man who's HIV positive. I understood him in this, though it did nothing for my esteem.

I laid my head to his shoulder in silence. "The purpose of condoms," I said after gathering my thoughts. "Is to protect against pregnancy, HIV, and other STDs. When men and women meet and decide to take each other to bed, the condom is used to protect against all that he or she may have; all which neither one can say the other doesn't have. Neither of them can say that the other is clean. That is the very reason for condoms." I went on to him in that fashion for a time. "The fact you don't know makes it no safer," I concluded. "That being the case, you should be terrified of every woman you take to bed."

"As long as I have you," he said. "I'll never know the terror of taking another to bed." He made love to me, then, and there was no sense of fear or reluctance about it. That in itself made the experience explosive, for it spoke of his desire for the union, the pleasure he found, that the act wasn't just to placate or pacify.

The tension between us was lost that day. In the weeks to follow, our relationship had come back to where it had been. More pleasant for me in that the truth was known, and no longer did I fear his sudden attempts to fuck me raw. I like most that I no longer have to deceive the man I love. Such should never be in a relationship.

DEAR DIARY,

It's been months since my last entry. Now that I'm no longer victimizing people, there isn't much to write about. Life for me is fair. Kevin and I still hold strong to one another with no signs of letting go. He has gotten me back into college and supports my attempts to excel. He wants me as a team player in his corporate world. I feel secure in that he's expanded that aspect of his life to include me. His visions of comfort seems a likely reality. He has made purchase of a building and is currently renovating it to the standards of a mid-class diner, with aims of having two up and running within the next year.

As for me, I currently attend college for Cooking & Catering along with Interior Decoration & Design. At the time of my diagnosis, I could never imagine so positive an outcome. My life has more meaning and purpose now than it ever had. It has been Kevin's attempt, for the last month, to set things and have me speak at schools and hold conferences on AIDS awareness and prevention. I was seriously opposed to the notion of public speaking and revealing to the world my diagnosis. Kevin pointed out the trauma and state of depression associated with such, reminding me that a person of compassion would never wish that on another and should help prevent such in what way possible. I nearly laughed, considering how I'd been everything but compassionate– quite the opposite, in fact– in intentionally bringing Death to the lives of many. He is correct, however, and though I can never take back what I've done, I will speak to others and educate in ways of protection.

I asked where from had this idea come, and he said from me; the night I'd given him the lecture on the purpose of condoms, the night I'd convinced him to set aside his fear and have sex with me. He thinks I'll be a good spokesman for condoms. I have a savvy way of stressing their significance, he said, and is certain I can convince other as well. I didn't bother telling him that a condom is useless if one of the sharing participants has malicious intent. However, I'm scheduled to have my first conference on the subject tomorrow, at Savannah Tech, and I will surely mention the possible destruction to condoms. I've heard several conferences on HIV and malice intent is an unprecedented topic.

This is a far cry from where I started. I've taken a one-eighty turn with the matter of my diagnosis. I'm more nervous about tomorrow than I'd been in administering Death to people. I know my effort in speaking out is the right thing to do, but I feel no excitement; no heavy sense of anticipation as there was in bringing harm. I should feel good about the idea of helping others, but I don't. That's not to say I hate it or that I have regrets in the matter; my feelings are merely neutral. I thought never to use this diary again, having documented my experience with victims and having since moved beyond. But there's a flip side to every coin, two sides to every story. And having accounted the darker aspect, I will begin tomorrow with the positive. Who knows, maybe there will be something exciting to this lifestyle after all.

DEAR READER,

My name is Kevin. I will conclude Alez's Diary and publish it to the world. "Conclude" because she is unable, for she has passed away. "Publish" so the world will know the kind of people that's out there, that this virus can easily catch the unsuspecting. It had been my desire to have Alez speak to the public pertaining to this disease, but she died shortly after her first conference. With her diary in print, its material raw and uncut, even in death she will bring home the message to many.

Alez died at my side as I knew she would someday, for I never intended to be without her. My love for her was genuine, and according to passages in her diary, she felt it. Of this I'm glad, for she was a jewel to have, and I wanted first and foremost her happiness. I've known for a while that she loved me, but only from her written passages did I know to what degree. Alez was angry, and I'm happy to have been spared her wrath. It was, however, that very same anger that brought about her demise.

Alez died holding my hand, her death a result of the virus she carried, but not in the sense that immediately comes to mind. Her death came in a manner that left me sick for days. She and I were walking through Savannah Tech's parking lot discussing her experience in having spoken before so large an audience when, out of nowhere, a brown Grand Prix sped up with bellowing pipes and stopped directly in front of us. The driver never looked at me. He had eyes only for Alez. There was something of an angry snarl to his face. A chrome 9mm was aimed out the window and fired twice before either one of us could act.

Alez fell backwards as the car sped away. I caught and lowered her to the ground, cradling her head in my lap. She was dead already, having been caught by both rounds in the face. I wept on the spot. It's something I wish not to stress in writing, but it hurt unlike anything in life. There can never be another like her. None could ever take her place. On some level I wish it not as true, for it makes my loss lifelong.

I thought, initially, the perpetrator had been a jealous ex-lover. I said this under police interrogation, minus the make and model of the car and the driver's description, those of which I withheld for personal reasons. To this I'll only say that no one has ever taken anything from me and has gotten away with it.

It wasn't until I discovered Alez's diary that I knew her killer was a victim within the pages of her manuscript. I need not say who, for you are just as capable as I in figuring that person's identity. Most would say Alez was evil and got what she deserved, but I can assure you the woman she portrayed herself to be isn't the woman I knew.

She was beautiful in mind and body. Her personality was magnetic. In fact, it was her personality and aura which drew her victims. She was a treasure to behold, and one simply wanted to possess her. The sense went beyond physical.

So different in life was Alez from the character within these pages that, upon stumbling across her diary, my first impression was that I held in hand an excellently crafted work of fiction. Then I recognized scenarios therein which could be none other than the truth. I don't condone what Alez has done. She was angry and what she did was wrong. Even so, it changes not my love for her. She was disturbed and saddened by her diagnosis and I'm glad to have restored some balance. She is gone now. Forever lost to me. Forever lost to the world…

So here lies the conclusion of Alez's diary, her Circle of Death. If you are reading this, the publishing process has been a success. Said names herein have been changed to protect the− what? Victims? Innocent? If you recognize yourself in these pages, or someone you've been sexually involved with, go get tested− your partner should go as well. Remember: protection is useless if one of the participants bears malice.

Broken Trust {Excerpt}

Ashley Rowan lay in bed fearfully awaiting the inevitable. She glanced at the bedside clock: 2:03 a.m. He was late, she thought. Maybe he wouldn't come home tonight. With her luck, fate would never allow that to happen. He would show for certain, to inflict pain, to torture.

"Please, Lord," Ashley prayed aloud for the umpteenth time within the last hour. "Give me this night alone." Her prayers to God were less frequent of late, her faith having fallen near the wayside. She called to him this night, however, as she had done many times before, seeking refuge from the treacherous hand of torture.

The distant slam of the front door resounded throughout the house.

"God, please!" Ashley pleaded with all her heart, willing her Father to oblige. She once knew serenity in coming to the Lord and having offered up her burden in prayer, but there was only fear now, a wrenched gut and a quickened pulse.

Although her room door was shut and locked from the outside, the house was quiet, and his heavy tread vibrated audibly up the hall, slow, deliberate, and tantalizing. A terror inducing tact, she recognized, and he took pleasure in the act. Of this she was certain.

His tread was silent now, strumming the chords of

agonizing suspense. Would he retire to his own room, sparing her a night's torment, or would he barge in and do to her all the things normal men didn't do to women? The suspense was strategically drawn out at times, boosting her terror to incapacitating heights.

There came the faint but unmistakable scrape of a key sliding into the door lock, pins clicking in place, and the thud or a thrown bolt. Terror-enhanced, the noise was ominous, and the door swinging open with James' menacing figure silhouetted against the hall's light was foreboding....

Kassidy is released after a year in juvenile, but he is welcomed home with violence and war. When one of his best friends is gunned down right in front of him, it is up to Kassidy and his street gang to find out who did it and why.

As Kassidy's rap career rise to new heights, the structure of people built around him screams success– until his past resurfaces during his first performance, forcing another change.

Follow the story of a teenager as he wades through a web of violence, heartbreak, and disloyalty in search of love, revenge, and justice. The conflict here is as strong as the twists are sharp!

Order at: www.tmapublishing.com

Or mail $15.00 check or money order to:
TMA Publishing
1915 E. Victory Square Drive Suite E#1009
Savannah, GA 31404

BROKEN TRUST

Thomas Habersham

Paranormal visions deliver the truth: Trayon's fiancée, Ashley Rowan has a secret lover. Torn by the reality, Trayon falls to old habits, and a blatant disregard for the law lands him an untimely death–from which he returns. The visions return as well, bringing impending flashes of doom...

Trapped by a madman and often under physical attacks, Ashley Rowan reluctantly submits to the man holding her captive. She is handled with care as a result, and the physical abuse seem a thing of the past. Then clarity reveals a terrifying truth that sparks a vicious fight of another kind.

Love, life, and death hangs in precarious balance. What's truly at stake, however, is more terrifying than either.

Order at: www.tmapublishing.com

Or mail $15.00 check or money order to:
TMA Publishing
1915 E. Victory Square Drive Suite E#1009
Savannah, GA 31404

You never think it will happen to you, that it will land on your doorstep– until it does. Now you can't believe it. Columnist, Dorothy Legler, has drawn the eyes of a deadly kidnapper. A terrifying world unfolds as people she knows turn up missing and those around her have questionable motives. With daring taunts and bold kidnappings, the stalker plays cat and mouse with Topeka Police.

When an officer disappears in the line of duty, and the Feds arrive with lead agent "Hound Dog" Rawls, it's clear Dorothy is Key to one, Target to the other, and the authorities are up against a criminal who is just as deadly as he is cunning. How many victims will be taken before the kidnapper is stopped? Will he be stopped? Or will he snatch the Target before the "Hound" has a chance to unlock his identity?

www.ingramcontent.com/pod-product-compliance
Lightning Source LLC
Chambersburg PA
CBHW051519170626
46811CB00002B/896